IN A WAR, YOU SPILL BLOOD

☆

Chapman was right, mused Torn. These *vaqueros* weren't bad men. They were ordinary cowboys, doing a job their boss had told them to do. Good soldiers, who didn't ask for reasons why.

But this was war, and a man did what he had to in order to live. That meant killing the men who were trying to kill you, and good or bad didn't enter into the equation.

Twenty yards. Almost across the river.

Cold, calm, deliberate, Torn drew a bead on one of the *vaqueros* riding at the point of the wedge and squeezed the trigger . . .

Also by Hank Edwards

THE JUDGE

WAR CLOUDS

GUN GLORY

TEXAS FEUD

STEEL JUSTICE

LAWLESS LAND

BAD BLOOD

RIVER RAID

Published by
HARPERPAPERBACKS

ATTENTION: ORGANIZATIONS AND CORPORATIONS

Most HarperPaperbacks are available at special quantity discounts for bulk purchases for sales promotions, premiums, or fund-raising. For information, please call or write:
Special Markets Department, HarperCollins Publishers,
10 East 53rd Street, New York, N.Y. 10022.
Telephone: (212) 207-7528. Fax: (212) 207-7222.

HANK EDWARDS

THE JUDGE

BORDER WAR

HarperPaperbacks
A Division of HarperCollinsPublishers

If you purchased this book without a cover, you should be aware that this book is stolen property. It was reported as "unsold and destroyed" to the publisher and neither the author nor the publisher has received any payment for this "stripped book."

This is a work of fiction. The characters, incidents, and dialogues are products of the author's imagination and are not to be construed as real. Any resemblance to actual events or persons, living or dead, is entirely coincidental.

HarperPaperbacks *A Division of* HarperCollins*Publishers*
10 East 53rd Street, New York, N.Y. 10022

Copyright © 1993 by HarperCollins*Publishers*
All rights reserved. No part of this book may be used or reproduced in any manner whatsoever without written permission of the publisher, except in the case of brief quotations embodied in critical articles and reviews. For information address HarperCollins*Publishers*,
10 East 53rd Street, New York, N.Y. 10022.

Cover illustration by Bill Maughan

First printing: March 1993

Printed in the United States of America

HarperPaperbacks and colophon are trademarks of HarperCollins*Publishers*

10 9 8 7 6 5 4 3 2 1

CHAPTER 1

THE DUSTY TEXAS BORDER TOWN OF EAGLE PASS WAS waking to a new day when death came thundering across the Rio Grande.

Eagle Pass had always been a quiet, peace-loving community. Its inhabitants were proud of the town's law-and-order reputation. They were hardworking, God-fearing folk, and they did not envy the wild and woolly character of nearby Laredo and El Paso.

By all accounts, a bright future lay in store for Eagle Pass. Productive mines had been established in the vicinity. The Coronado Cattle Company and the Sierra Vista ranch were flourishing. Eagle Pass serviced the needs of the miners and the cowboys, and kept these lusty rowdies in line by employing quick-fisted badge toters who were just as quick with their guns when fists weren't enough to keep the peace.

The Texas Pacific Railroad had put a branch line

down to Eagle Pass and built a depot. More prosperity was pouring along the iron road into town. The army had established Camp Warren on the other side of Indio Wash from the community, and stationed elements of the Third Cavalry there.

The future was definitely bright for Eagle Pass, Texas.

Until Garza Santiago and his outlaw army struck.

The citizens of Eagle Pass were well aware that trouble was brewing south of the border. Trouble was always brewing down there. The government was brutal and oppressive, spawning rebel groups that were led for the most part by men who were just as brutal and oppressive as the government. These bandit leaders were using the cruel tyranny of Mexico's president, Porfirio Díaz, as an excuse to raid, loot, and pillage small villages. As usual, it was the common people who suffered.

Prior to the raid on Eagle Pass, these rebel bandits had limited their depredations to the Mexican side of the Rio Grande.

In the aftermath of the raid, no one could make sense of this unbelievable outrage. American soil had been invaded by an armed and hostile force for the first time since the British had landed during the War of 1812.

Some assumed Santiago was tired of the slim pickings found in poor Mexican towns—that the brimming coffers of the Eagle Pass *nortistas* drew him like the church bells drew the faithful on Sabbath morning. Others—those who mistook Santiago for someone who gave a damn about the revolution—argued that the raid was retaliation for the United States's tacit support of the Díaz regime.

Only later did the real reason for the raid on Eagle

Pass come to light: a conspiracy involving guns and gold.

The truth became known because a handful of brave men were willing to put their lives on the line to get at it.

One of those men was Clay Torn, who just happened to be in Eagle Pass, visiting an old friend, when Garza Santiago and his killers came calling.

CHAPTER 2

CAMP WARREN WAS FOREWARNED.

Colonel Edgar P. Dalworth, commanding officer, knuckled sleep out of his eyes while listening to the hysterical blatherings of the vaquero Lieutenant Chapman had brought before him.

A twenty-year veteran, Dalworth prided himself on being cool and collected in times of crisis. He did not, however, deem this to be a crisis. As a result, he did not feel compelled to exercise calm detachment. Especially since he had been rousted out of bed at . . . what the hell time was it, anyway? He reached for the stemwinder customarily fobbed across his tunic, only to realize that in his haste he had managed to don only his trousers and boots. From the waist up he was clothed in a pin-striped nightshirt. Having to present himself in this half-dressed condition did not improve his disposition, and he fixed a withering glower upon the young shavetail who was to blame for this middle-of-the-night intrusion.

"Chapman," he rasped, exasperated, "will you shut him up?"

The Mexican was rattling on, scarcely pausing to draw breath, and gesturing wildly.

"Yes, sir." Chapman addressed the vaquero in excellent Spanish, interrupting him in midsentence.

"Thank God," breathed the cross Dalworth. "Peace and quiet."

"Not for long, Colonel, if what this man says is true."

"And what exactly *is* he saying, Lieutenant?"

"He claims that yesterday he and four other riders employed by the Coronado Cattle Company were out in the brush about twenty miles south of the border, hunting strays. They were accompanied by Frank Robles."

Dalworth nodded. He knew Robles, the Coronado foreman.

"They were sitting down to supper," continued Chapman, "when suddenly they found their camp surrounded by *garcistas*. Rebels who follow Garza Santiago, sir."

"Rebels?" Dalworth grunted. "Bandits, you mean. How many?"

"He says there were over a hundred."

Dalworth was skeptical. "Which means that in fact there were only ten or twenty."

Chapman shrugged. "Santiago ordered his men to hang them all."

"Hang them? What the devil for?"

"To save on ammunition, sir. Santiago didn't want any of them to get away and spread an alarm."

Dalworth peered at the Coronado vaquero. Dark and tough as old leather, but at closer glance hardly more than a boy. He wore a *chaqueta* and leather *chivarras*. A braided *cuerta* dangled from his wrist. Born and raised in the *monte*. Wasn't much could scare one such as this. But he was shaken. Scared clean through. In the end Dalworth did not believe his story. He did not have a very high opinion of Mexicans. They were too emotional, too prone to exaggerate.

"Seems Santiago's plan went awry. Do you believe him, Lieutenant?"

Lips pursed, Chapman took a long look at the Coronado rider. "I'm not sure, sir."

"I don't believe this youngster escaped a hundred bandits, I can tell you that," said Dalworth.

The colonel crossed the rustic parlor of his quarters, moving closer to the stone hearth. He tried to kick last night's embers into life, but all he got for his effort was a blemish of ash on his spit-and-polish boots. About to call for his orderly, he remembered it was the middle of the night. He grimaced. The chill got into his bones, aggravated his arthritis.

"Hell," he groused. "I've had this assignment for almost one year, Lieutenant. We patrol two hundred miles of border, day in and day out. I don't know how many false reports of this nature I've heard in that time. Not one amounted to anything. Not a single one." He hawked night-gather and spat into the blackened maw of the fireplace. Then he sighed. "You woke me for nothing, Chapman. Even if what this fellow says is true, there's little we can do about it. We can't cross the border."

"It's been done, sir," said Chapman. "By other units."

"But not by this one, dammit. Every time an army patrol ventures south of the border, there's hell to pay. The Díaz government kicks up an unholy fuss."

"Our War Department is trying to get Díaz to sign

the Hot Trail Treaty. That would permit us to cross over into Mexico as long as we're in pursuit of—"

"By God, Lieutenant, you don't have to tell me what our War Department is doing!" Dalworth was indignant. "But the fact remains they haven't done it yet."

"He says he overheard the bandits discussing Eagle Pass."

"What are you getting at?"

"Nothing, sir. Just relaying what he said."

"They can discuss Boston, Massachusetts, as far as I'm concerned. Just so long as they stay the hell off American soil."

"Yes, sir."

"See that he has food and coffee. And get him the hell out of here so I can get some sleep."

After Chapman and the vaquero had gone, Dalworth moodily paced the parlor for five minutes, having second thoughts about discounting the suggestion that Garza Santiago's outlaw army bore any threat to the town of Eagle Pass.

Santiago was a daring and ruthless bandit. He was terrorizing Mexican villages on the other side of the Rio Grande. But Dalworth couldn't give much credence to the idea that Santiago would cross the river in force. The man wasn't *that* crazy.

Camp Warren's commanding officer went back to bed. It was a little after three in the morning. He slept well for another two hours.

He never again, for the rest of his life, slept that well.

As Colonel Dalworth went back to sleep a goatherd named Emiliano awoke and arose from his straw-tick mattress in a small hut two miles south of Camp Warren.

The hut consisted of one dirt-floored room and was

made of maguey bloom stalks, with a roof of clay on a matting of ocotillo. The old man had lived here for thirty years. Alone for the last ten.

He smoked an oak-leaf cigarette, a taste he had acquired thanks to his long-dead wife, a Lipan Apache woman. Somewhere out in the night his dog barked—barked three times and then no more. A moment later Emiliano felt the earth tremble beneath his bare feet, and before long the incessant drumroll of a thousand hooves filled his ears.

Emiliano crossed himself and stepped out of the hut, prepared to die.

Dust stirred, like the powder of crushed bones. His eyes deeply embedded in a walnut-brown face as fissured as the surface of an alkali flat, Emiliano looked at the mass of mounted men encircling his hut, dark and featureless shapes against a star-bright sky. Hard-run horses blew steam in the brisk predawn air.

"What is your name, *anciano?*"

Emiliano answered truthfully, addressing them all, as he was unsure which had spoken.

"Who else lives here?"

"No one. I am alone."

"A lonely old man, eh?"

"I am not alone. I have my goats, and my dog."

Someone laughed—a harsh, ruffian sound.

"You will have to get another dog. One that does not make so much noise."

Emiliano merely nodded. He had buried many dogs.

"The gringos in the town north of here. Do you know them?"

"Some of them."

"Are they your friends, old man?"

Some were. Sometimes Emiliano would sell a *cordero* or two in Eagle Pass. He used the proceeds to buy parched corn for coffee, and occasionally splurged on a stick of licorice.

But Emiliano had not seen ninety-five years by taking sides. "I only know them," he replied, in the noncommittal way of peasants everywhere.

"Maybe you should ride with us, eh?"

"I am too old to fight."

"He is too old for anything," came a new voice. "He is a worthless bag of bones. I say kill him."

"No. I think he will live a long time yet," said the man who had done most of the talking. "Longer than we will, *compadre.*"

Gruff laughter rippled through the shadow riders.

Something flickered starlight and landed in the dust at Emiliano's feet.

"Buy yourself a new dog, *anciano*. Compliments of Garza Santiago. Name him after me. *Ojala, muchachos!*"

Then they were gone, their thunder quickly dwindling.

Emiliano picked up the coin. He turned it over and over with gnarled but nimble fingers. *Nortista* money, a double eagle—twenty-dollar gold piece. He licked the coin and nodded. Pure gold. He knew the taste of pure gold.

CHAPTER 3

HEARING DISTANT THUNDER, MEG SLAUGHTER ROSE FROM her bed and went to the window. The floor was cold underfoot, and she walked on tiptoe with the willowy grace of a ballerina.

Parting the curtains, she peered out. Rugged peaks stood in stark relief against the gray filament of false dawn lining the desert's eastern rim. She thought they looked like black teeth tearing at the sky. The stars were out in all their glory, and she saw no evidence of storm clouds gathering. The thunder faded. How curious.

From the window of her second-story bedroom, Meg could look out over most of Eagle Pass. The town still slept. She looked for smoke from the chimneys of other houses and saw none. But beyond the rooftops she *could* see a cloud of pale dust hugging the earth like a small patch of fog. She pressed the palm of her hand against a pane of glass. Not the slightest vibration. No wind to speak of. Why, then, the dust?

Her reflection in the glass drew her attention, capturing her sleepy smile. She used both hands to sweep thick, tawny, pillow-mussed hair from her face. The lift of her slender arms pulled the soft cotton of her nightdress taut across her breasts. The frigid kiss of the winter chill made her nipples stand out.

Feeling delightfully wicked, she wondered what her father would say if he knew she was exposing herself at a window in her unmentionables. What a shameless hussy! This was no way for the daughter of Burton Slaughter to act. She was too pretty for her own good, said he. And she wasn't demure enough to satisfy him. But she was no gentle southern belle, as her mother had been. She'd been born in the Old South, true enough, but raised in the West. My little tomboy, Burton Slaughter called her, with pride poorly concealed behind the gentle censure.

Was she too pretty? She bent closer to the window and examined the starlit image with a critical eye. She didn't think so. But then she wasn't a man, and men positively dropped their teeth when they saw her. It was a little embarrassing, the way they fawned over her. Flattering, too. She tried to act shy, but that was flying false colors and made her feel like a flirt. She was vivacious and bold and full of life, and she liked the attention. She wasn't really a tomboy anymore. She was a woman, with a woman's needs.

No, she really didn't think of herself as pretty, because she judged feminine beauty by the portrait of her mother hanging on the wall in the parlor downstairs. Her mother had been pale and delicate. Meg was sun dark and wiry. It was a good thing, she thought, that women were scarce out here. She wouldn't get a second glance in New Orleans or Charleston, but in Eagle Pass she was the belle of the ball.

Yes, she liked the attention. Did that make her a bad girl? She thought not. But if so, so be it. What was wrong with smiling back at a man when he smiled at her? It amused her when these tough westerners began to blush and stammer like schoolboys in her presence. Lieutenant Oliver Chapman came immediately to mind. In spite of his youth, Oliver had a reputation as a fearless fighter, proven in a dozen engagements against Mexican bandits and renegade Indians. Yet when he came around her, he looked positively terrified. She smiled warmly at the thought of him.

Then she thought about Clay Torn, and the smile disappeared. Studying her reflection in the window glass, she realized that suddenly she looked a little terrified. Torn was asleep in a room across the hall—and that was why she was having a difficult time sleeping.

What was it about that man?

He was an old friend of her father's, and he had stopped by for a visit. He and her father had fought together during the war. They had saved each other's lives. There was a bond—a very strong and enduring bond—between them.

Torn's last visit had been four years ago. He had come and gone without making much of an impression on Meg, then fourteen years old. Four years ago she had been a tomboy.

This time, though, he was making a very deep impression on her.

She wasn't sure why. It was all very disturbing. He did not pay her the kind of attention other men did. He did not follow her around like a little lost puppy, the way Chapman, for instance, was prone to do. He smiled back when she smiled at him, but it was a painfully polite smile, a slightly sad smile.

He was a handsome man, in a dark and dangerous way. Grim and hard and taciturn, he had a reputation as a killer. She knew he was a federal judge, and she knew about Melony Hancock.

Torn had been engaged to Melony at the outbreak of the War between the States, and he had returned home to South Carolina only to find his family dead, his home destroyed, and his fiancée vanished. He had been searching for her ever since—more than ten years now. It was all so very tragic. Like something out of Shakespeare. Meg's heart went out to him. It was a hopeless quest; everyone knew it, except Torn himself. He refused to give up. Like one of Arthur's Round Table knights, seeking the Holy Grail.

Torn had taken a leave of absence from his duties as a federal judge to travel to Santa Fe, following a lead he had hoped would reunite him with his long-lost love. Of course, it had been a false lead. He had stopped off in Eagle Pass, on his way to Brownsville and a steamer bound for New Orleans, whence he would take a riverboat up the Mississippi to St. Louis.

Meg knew he was going to leave in a few days, and for some reason she couldn't bear the thought of another few years passing before she could see him again. She knew also that his love for Melony was so strong that there was no room in his heart for another woman.

So why, with every bachelor in Eagle Pass after her, was she so infatuated with a man she could not have?

Shivering, she scurried back to bed, slipping beneath the covers and pulling them over her head. The tip of her nose, and her bare feet, were frozen. She kept thinking about Torn, in the room across the hall, and warmed up. He had promised, finally, to take her riding today. She felt a little guilty; before Torn's arrival she had promised to spend part of the day with Oliver. But Chapman wasn't going anywhere, and in a few days Clay Torn would be gone.

Tomorrow might be her last chance.

She wished the sun would hurry.

CHAPTER 4

TORN HAD A NIGHTMARE, AND MELONY HANCOCK WAS IN IT.
She was standing far off across a sagebrush flat, her arms held out to him, and she was calling, calling his name, or so it seemed. He couldn't be certain because he couldn't hear her above the thunder of horses on the run. Behind her, raising a cloud of angry, swirling dust as pale as a dead man's flesh, were four riders. They were clad all in black, and he couldn't make out their features. He knew he ought to be able to see them clearly; it was daylight in his dream. But the four riders did not have faces. Their horses were exhaling steam, and galloping straight for Melony. Her back was to the four riders. Surely she heard them coming. But she paid them no heed. Faintly, above the deafening drumroll of the horses' hooves, Torn could hear the chiming of a church bell.

The four riders weren't going to turn aside. They

were bent on riding Melony down. They were going to kill her. Torn knew he could save her. He could reach her in time, could pull her out of harm's way. All he had to do was run to her.

Instead, sensing someone behind him, he turned—to find Meg Slaughter standing there.

A strong wind was blowing, and her tawny hair was streaming. The wind molded the thin, gossamer gown she was wearing to her willowy young body, and Torn could see every desirable curve—she might as well have been wearing nothing at all. Her sea-green eyes were bright with passion, her lips were wet and slightly parted.

Before he knew it, he was in her arms, bruising her lips with his, and he could feel every inch of her long supple body pressing eagerly against him. The world went into a spin. He looked up and was facing toward Melony again. Hot shame swept through him. Melony was weeping bitterly. She covered her face with her hands and dropped to her knees. And then the four riders were upon her. She disappeared between flashing hooves. A guttural cry escaped Torn's lips, the bone-chilling wail of a wounded animal. The four riders were coming on, coming straight for him now, and he reached for the Colt Peacemaker in the holster on his hip.

He awoke, sitting upright in bed, shivering. He was drenched with sweat, and the night was cold. Normally he slept with the Colt under his pillow. He found the Peacemaker now in his hand, the hammer back, his finger on the trigger. Looking around the room, he remembered where he was. The nightmare was over. Yet he could still hear the thunder of horses at the gallop.

Shaken, he kicked free of the covers twisted around his legs and rolled out of bed. Clad in long johns, the

Colt in hand, he went to the window and parted the curtains. The street below was quiet. Eagle Pass was sleeping. False dawn lightened the eastern sky. Not a single cloud blotted out the still-bright stars. So why the unending thunder?

Feeling drained, weak at the knees, he leaned against the wall, brushed wheat-colored hair out of his steel-gray eyes. He was a tall, lean man in his midthirties. A hard life had made him a hard man, physically and mentally. But, like everyone, he had moments of weakness.

It was just a dream.

Yet he couldn't convince himself, because deep down inside he knew there was more to it.

He was giving up hope of ever finding Melony.

A dozen years he had searched, to no avail. Finding her had become an obsession. Now, it seemed, he was losing the will to go on. Reality was setting in.

Maybe it was the long trip to Santa Fe, and the despair he had experienced upon discovering that it had been for naught . . . though it wasn't the first false lead he had followed to its bitter end. More like the hundredth. He'd lost count. But he had the feeling it was going to be the last.

He carried a photograph of Melony, a daguerreotype taken on the eve of his departure for the war, and over the years he had shown it to thousands of people. A few months ago, in Wichita, he had shown it to a cattleman up from New Mexico with a herd to sell. The rancher said he had seen a woman who looked remarkably similar. He couldn't swear to it, but . . .

A slim chance, but Torn had had to take it. Melony had been eighteen when the photograph was taken. Almost seventeen years had passed. People changed, and remarkably similar was close enough.

The woman the cattleman had seen lived a reclusive life on one of the biggest spreads in New Mexico; it had been a Spanish land grant, and the owner, the woman's husband, came from a long line of grandees.

It had proven to be a long ride for nothing.

Why was it, Torn wondered, that after all this time, after so many false leads, he still couldn't prepare himself for the disappointment?

I can't go on like this.

It was hopeless. Perhaps he'd known that all along, and was just now accepting it.

A man needed a home, a wife, a family. If he didn't have these things, he wasn't a whole man. Torn had passed on several opportunities; there were a few women scattered along his back trail who had loved him, and whom he could have loved. But he had remained faithful to Melony, and moved on.

He glanced across the darkened room at the door to the hallway and thought about Meg Slaughter asleep in the room across the way. She was interested in him, that much he could tell. Maybe it wasn't love. Maybe it was. He hadn't been paying her much attention—old habits died hard—but he wanted to. What if she was his last chance for happiness?

Tomorrow, then, he would let his defenses down, before it was too late.

And then the shooting started.

CHAPTER 5

ON THE DARK DESERT PLAIN BETWEEN CAMP WARREN AND Eagle Pass, Garza Santiago halted his army of two hundred bandits. He nodded curtly to Ochoa, his most trusted lieutenant. A nod was all that was needed. Everything had been planned beforehand, down to the last detail.

Ochoa took a hundred and fifty men west, toward the army camp. The balance followed Santiago to the edge of town. It was Ochoa's job to keep the Yankee soldiers busy while Santiago performed the task he had come so far, and been so well paid, to do.

Again, on the outskirts of Eagle Pass, Santiago called a brief halt. He looked about him, scanning the dark faces of the men who followed his lead. Their eyes were bright with anticipation. This was what they had been born to do. Kill, loot, rape, destroy. They lived for it.

Died for it. Santiago grinned. This was what made life worth living.

He called out six names. "You men will stay with me. The rest of you, do your worst. Kill as many gringos as you can. Take as much as you can carry. Make them pay for sleeping in the same bed with that bastard Díaz." Then he added, wryly, "Viva Mexico."

Some of the men laughed. They knew Santiago was joking. They had no illusions. The so-called revolution was their license to commit crime.

"Viva Santiago!" The cry shattered the stillness of dawn. Big-roweled Chihuahua spurs bit deep, and their horses, snorting, lunged into a gallop. Santiago kept his mount under tight rein as the bandits swept past. He and the six men he had handpicked waited until the shooting started before heading straight for the house of Burton Slaughter.

Lieutenant Oliver Chapman had just returned to the officer-of-the-day's hut, having made his last round of the sentry posts, when the bandits struck Camp Warren.

His first thought, when he heard the shooting, was that Dalworth was a gold-plated fool.

The colonel had not taken seriously enough the story told by the Coronado vaquero. Chapman had decided that in Dalworth's shoes he would have called the post to arms. Better safe than sorry. Dalworth might at least have ordered a doubling of the night guard. And he hadn't even thought to advise anyone in Eagle Pass of the possible threat.

Bolting out of the hut with his Army Colt in hand, Chapman looked to his left. Private Rheiss was posted at the southwest corner of the camp, near the commissary. He saw Rheiss standing his ground, firing his

Spencer carbine into the night gloom still gathered in the depths of Indio Wash. Suddenly Rheiss dropped the Spencer and performed a jerky dance as a hail of bullets ripped him apart.

Like a tidal wave of death, dozens of horsemen emerged from the wash and poured into the compound, howling "Viva Mexico!" and "Viva Santiago!", their guns spitting flame.

Chapman spun on his heel and ran past the guardhouse and hospital, making for the barracks on the east side of the parade ground. Above the din of battle he heard a horse running hard right behind him. He looked over his shoulder, still sprinting full stride. One of the bandits was after him. The Mexican aimed his pistol at Chapman's back. The lieutenant dived left, across the path of the horse, rolled, and came up in a crouch, agile as a cat. The bandit cursed; he had to bring his gun across his body and over the neck of his horse, and before he could accomplish that, Chapman shot him out of the saddle.

Chapman lunged for the riderless horse, got a hand on a saddle fender, but lost his grip and ate dirt. He felt better about things when he was on a horse. He fought better in the saddle, with the reins in his teeth, a saber in one hand and a gun in the other. Hell, if he'd wanted to fight on foot, he would have joined the infantry. He'd spent his whole life on the back of a cayuse. His father had been a mustanger, and Chapman had learned to ride before he learned to walk. It had seemed a natural use of his equestrian talents to join the cavalry. He rode like a Comanche.

Troopers were spilling out of the barracks to exchange fire with the bandits, now milling around on the parade ground. Chapman was running again, firing into the mass of attackers. His revolver was empty by the time he reached the barracks. Two bandits came out of the maelstrom of dust, heading straight for him. A trooper, Hanrahan, saw Chapman and yelled a warning, firing his Spencer at the same time. One of the bandits somersaulted off his horse. The other shot Hanrahan twice in the chest. Chapman tossed his empty Colt away, drew his saber, turned, and charged, yelling at the top of his lungs.

He had long ago made himself a promise: when he died in battle, as he somehow knew he would, he would be going forward.

Chapman's audacity caught the bandit by surprise. He tightened up on the reins so suddenly that the horse beneath him reared. That threw off the bandit's aim. The one shot he fired at Chapman went wide. Chapman's saber amputated the Mexican's gun arm six inches above the wrist. The bandit howled and toppled out of the saddle. The lieutenant was moving in to finish the job when a bullet hit him high in the shoulder, knocking him down.

Stunned, Chapman lay there a moment, facedown in the dirt, and the battle raged on about him. He felt cold and numb—no pain, yet. Three troopers advanced into the fray to reach his side. While two lay down a covering fire the third tried to drag Chapman in the direction of the barracks. Chapman resisted.

"I can walk, thank you very much," he snapped.

The trooper grinned, glad to see the lieutenant alive. A split second later a bullet hit him right between the eyes.

Chapman got to his feet and stumbled to the barracks. The two troopers covered his back. Shouting to be heard above the din of battle, he ordered the cavalrymen back inside the buildings. The Spencer carbine took a seven-shot tubular magazine; Chapman picked several men to serve as ammo bearers. Their job was to keep the troopers at the doors and windows supplied. Colonel Dalworth had wanted to keep the carbines and ammunition in an armory under lock and key; that was the way they did things back east. Chapman thanked God the man had listened to reason. Out here you slept with your weapons if you wanted to survive.

Protected by adobe walls two feet thick, the troopers lay down a withering fire. Chapman told the men to pick their targets. To make certain every bullet counted. He admired their coolness under fire. The tide of battle was turning—he could feel it. In a matter of minutes the gunfire diminished. The troopers let go with a ragged cheer as the bandits quit the compound.

Chapman was the first man out of the barracks. The cloud of dust and gun smoke slowly lifted to reveal a parade ground littered with dead and dying men and horses. Troopers ran to help wounded friends. Others ventured out among the enemy casualties. Chapman saw one cavalryman finish off a wounded bandit with a bullet in the skull. The lieutenant grimly turned away.

Then he saw the black plume of smoke off in the distance. His blood ran cold.

Eagle Pass was under attack.

Meg . . .

He headed for the stables in a shuffling run. The ground tilted sharply; he stumbled and fell. White-hot pain lanced through him. He'd forgotten about the bullet in his arm. The sleeve of his tunic was soaked with blood. He tried to get up, but the world began to spin, faster and faster, and he couldn't find the strength. The spirit was willing, but the body had taken enough punishment.

He closed his eyes and passed out.

CHAPTER 6

FROM THE WINDOW OF HIS ROOM ON THE SECOND FLOOR OF Burton Slaughter's house, Torn watched mounted men appear suddenly in the street below, emerging from the dawn's gray gloom like ghosts, dashing this way and that on their stretched-out mounts. The morning's peace and quiet was rudely shattered by the crash of gunfire.

An icy calm took hold of Torn. It came from experience. He had come under fire many times during the war and been shot at since then more times than he could count. He had learned that the single most important aid to survival was keeping one's wits. Too many men stopped thinking and started reacting when the guns spoke—an often fatal mistake.

They were Mexican bandits. He could gather as much by their garb and their shouts. He didn't wonder what they were doing on American soil; plenty of time to wonder about that later, if he lived. They were here, and they were doing their worst, shooting out windows, breaking in doors, killing and looting.

Slaughter's house was one of seven residences on the west side of the street. On the other side were two more homes, two stores, the Commercial Hotel, and a livery. Torn spent only a moment at the window, sizing up the enemy before deciding on a course of action—a habit of a good soldier. In that time he saw two Mexicans stampede a half-dozen horses out of the livery yard. Several more came out of the stores loaded up to the eyebrows with loot. At the end of the street, two more bandits dragged a woman out of one of the houses. Torn grimaced. The range was too great for his Colt. He was about to fetch his Winchester long gun when the woman, fighting like a wildcat, broke free. Her nightdress in tattered shreds, she began to run. One of the Mexicans shot her in the back.

"Bastard," muttered Torn.

He turned back into the room, pulled on trousers and boots, stuck the Colt under his belt. The Winchester leaned against the wall next to the bed. He snatched it up and returned to the window.

It was time for the sinners to pay for their sins.

A half-dozen bandits had converged on the Commercial, almost directly across the street from the Slaughter house. Using coal oil taken from the stores, some doused the walls and front gallery while others blazed away at the windows. With a roar, the gallery burst into flames. From inside the hotel a woman screamed, an infant cried—sounds that set Torn's teeth on edge. He tore the curtains down and used the Winchester's brass-plated butt to smash the window. His first shot knocked a bandit out of the saddle. His second hurled another Mexican into the blazing inferno of the gallery.

It wasn't a killing shot; the bandit lived long enough to become a human torch, writhing and wailing in agony.

"Better get used to burning," said Torn.

A bandit spotted him, yelled to his *compañeros,* and a flurry of hot lead demolished what was left of the window. Torn threw himself to the floor. He had placed the Slaughters in even greater jeopardy by drawing the attention of the raiders to this house, and now the first order of business was getting Burton and Meg to safety. Like most of the Americans who had come to Eagle Pass, Burton had built his home with lumber brought in by wagon from the distant sierra, spurning the use of adobe. In this climate, clapboard buildings burned like tinderboxes. Fully expecting the raiders to put the Slaughter residence to the torch, Torn realized there was no time to waste. The house, on the edge of town, backed up to Indio Wash. If he could get the Slaughters safely to the wash, they could lay low out in the desert brush until the danger had passed.

Once Burton and his daughter were out of harm's way, Torn resolved to come back and take issue with the bandits again. The odds didn't deter him. He was accustomed to facing long odds.

When Torn failed to return fire, the bandits in the street below stopped slinging lead at the bedroom window. Seizing the chance, Torn scrambled to his feet, grabbed his saber-knife, hanging in its custom-made shoulder harness on the bedpost, and went out into the hall. Meg was coming out of her room, pulling a flannel wrapper tight around her slender body. Burton was pounding up the stairs, barefoot and shirtless, a big barrel-chested man with craggy features and thinning hair the color of iron, a Davenport double-barrel shotgun in his hands.

"What the hell is going on?" he roared, scowling darkly.

"Got to get out of here," said Torn. "Take your daughter out the back. Hide in the brush."

"I'm not much for hiding, dammit."

Torn suppressed a smile. Burton was a hotheaded Irishman. Always had been, always would be. Torn deemed it a miracle that the man, with his firebrand ways, had survived the war.

"You've got Meg to think about," Torn reminded him.

"I'm a better shot than most men around here," said Meg.

"Like father, like daughter," said Torn, shaking his head. "Look. They're burning the town. Killing everybody they come across. No time to argue. Now, get the hell down those stairs and out the back way."

Burton took his daughter's arm. "Come on, Meg. When the colonel gives an order, he expects it to be carried out."

They hurried down the staircase. As they reached the bottom Torn heard boot heels thumping the front-porch planks. As Burton and Meg turned right, making for the back door, Torn turned left. The front door cracked back on its hinges. Torn fired the Winchester at hip level, dropping the first bandit through the door. Burton's shotgun roared. The blast of double-ought hurled another bandit backward, knocking two more off balance.

"Get her out of here!" Torn yelled at Burton. "I'll cover you."

Burton grabbed Meg and ran for the back door. Torn sent a few more rounds through the front door, backstepping as he fired. The two bandits on the front porch could do nothing but keep their heads down.

As Burton reached the back door it flew open, struck him, and sent him reeling.

"Father!" cried Meg.

Garza Santiago stepped through the doorway, two more bandits close behind.

"Buenos días, señorita," he said, grinning like a wolf.

CHAPTER 7

BURTON SLAUGHTER STILL HAD A BARRELFUL OF BUCKSHOT, and he was inclined to give it to Santiago. He was quick to recover—but not quite quick enough. One of Garza's companions stepped in to knock the shotgun aside a second before Slaughter pulled the trigger. Double-ought peppered the hall floor. The bandit clubbed Burton with his pistol. Slaughter collapsed, blood streaming down his face.

This time Meg screamed.

She was afraid for her father not for herself. She gave no thought whatever to her own safety. In her childhood she had run with the boys, and sometimes fought with them. She knew how to fight—something to which more than a few of the young men who had grown up in Eagle Pass could testify.

She lunged at the bandit who had hurt her father, and the Mexican had time to flash an ugly grin. After all, he was *mucho hombre,* and this was only a slim, weak, gringo girl. He thought it might be fun. A heartbeat later Meg had kneed him in the crotch and driven a fist into his vile, yellow grin. The man went down like cut timber, groping his private parts, spitting blood, and wheezing like a bellows.

Torn whirled when he heard the commotion at the back door. He saw Slaughter fall and witnessed the painful fate of the bandit who had incurred Meg's wrath. That left two Mexicans in the doorway. Two men standing between Meg and freedom. In a matter of seconds the two men he had been holding at bay on the front porch would come through and kill him. They'd shoot him in the back. It wouldn't matter to them. But Torn didn't let that deter him. He knew where his duty lay.

He brought the Winchester to bear on Santiago.

Garza saw it coming. Just as Torn lined up his shot the bandit leader lashed out, grabbed Meg by the hair, and pulled her roughly to him, a human shield. Meg struggled furiously—until Santiago jammed the barrel of his pistol under her chin and pulled the hammer back.

"Drop your weapons, hombre, or she dies."

Torn didn't hesitate. He had no doubt Santiago would carry out his threat. He was a dead man anyway—that much was certain. In this way at least he bought a little more time for Meg.

He tossed the Winchester away.

"The *pistola,* gringo. Slowly."

Torn plucked the Colt out of his belt with thumb and forefinger and threw it away as well. Behind him, the two bandits who, a moment ago, had been cowering on the front porch, charged through the doorway. Torn's spine crawled; his body tensed for the impact of a bullet.

"Don't kill him!" roared Santiago, and repeated the order in Spanish.

Torn did not know Garza Santiago. This wasn't his bailiwick—he was just passing through. All he knew about the so-called revolution in Mexico and the large-scale outlawry taking place all along what had come to be called the Bloody Border was what he had overheard or read in newspapers. But it was immediately clear to him that this man who was barking orders was the undisputed leader of these bandits.

And he was cunning like a fox.

Santiago was assuming—correctly, as it turned out—that Torn did not speak or comprehend much Spanish. That he had given the command in English as well as Spanish was significant, and even in such dire circumstances Torn was coolheaded enough to understand what was happening. Santiago was giving him hope for survival. He didn't want Torn to try something out of desperation. He wanted Torn alive.

But why?

Torn winced as one of Santiago's men jammed a gun barrel against his spine. He kept quite still, hands held out away from his sides.

Santiago handed Meg to the bandit in the doorway behind him. Meg was inclined to resume the fight, and there was a brief but fierce scuffle as she proceeded to give the *pistolero* trouble.

"Meg, be still," snapped Torn.

She complied. The bandit got one arm around her waist and hooked the other around her throat. He wasn't going to take any chances, having no wish to wind up groveling on the floor like his *compañero*. Meg didn't care much for his rough embrace, but she endured it, watching Torn, trusting him.

Santiago stepped closer to Torn. Tendrils of dawn

light had slipped into the hallway through the open doors, and Torn got his first good look at the bandit leader. Garza was a tall, wide-shouldered man who moved with a slow, almost lazy grace. But Torn was not deceived. Santiago could strike like lightning. Forged in the crucible of the desert, without an ounce of softness to him, he was as harsh and merciless as the land he roamed. No ordinary man could lead a pack of two-legged wolves like this bunch. As bad as these bandits were, Santiago was worse.

"Hombre, what is your name?" asked Garza, his eyes searching Torn's for a trace of fear.

He found none.

"Clay Torn. Yours?"

"You are a stranger here."

"Passing through."

"Wrong place at the wrong time, gringo."

The hint of a faintly insolent smile curled the corner of Torn's mouth.

"I don't see it that way."

Santiago stepped back a little. He looked Torn over from head to heels, and chuckled. *"Mucho hombre,* eh? I am Garza Santiago, and I fight for the freedom of the people, the poor campesinos who are being crushed beneath the heel of that tyrant Díaz."

"You're on the wrong side of the river, Santiago. Did you lose your way?"

"I go where I want, do what I want. And I take what I want. Your knife, for instance." He held out his hand. "Give it to me."

The saber-knife, in its harness, hung from Torn's shoulder.

"I'm kind of partial to it," said Torn. "So why don't you try taking it?"

CHAPTER 8

THE SABER-KNIFE WAS FIFTEEN INCHES OF TEMPERED STEEL with a single-guard hilt. It had once been a saber belonging to a Yankee sergeant named Karl Schmidt, a sadistic prison guard who had been obsessed with breaking Torn during the latter's sixteen months of living hell at the Point Lookout prisoner-of-war camp. Torn had acquired the saber during his escape—after using it to kill Schmidt. Later the blade had broken; Torn had fashioned what remained into a knife that was already famous on the frontier. Having it had been the difference between life and death for him at least a dozen times. It was his weapon of choice, and more. The Colt was just a pistol, the Winchester just a rifle. They could be replaced. But the saber-knife was a part of his past, a part of him, and he was not inclined to give it up without a fight.

Santiago's eyes, deep set in a hawkish but not unhandsome face, glittered with amusement at Torn's blunt refusal to render up the blade.

"You are a brave man. A brave man who is your enemy, he should be killed quick. It is a shame I must let you live." Santiago nodded at the body of Burton Slaughter. "And this one. Tell me his name."

Torn told him.

Santiago nodded. He stood there a moment, staring moodily at Slaughter. "I thought so," he said finally, and turned sharply on his heel.

The bandit who had pistol-whipped Slaughter and then suffered the full measure of Meg's wrath was still down, awash in a sea of pain. Santiago walked over to him.

"Raza, you are a fool," declared Garza, his voice pitched barely above a whisper.

Then he aimed his pistol at the bandit's head and squeezed the trigger.

A strangled noise escaped Meg as she witnessed the execution. Briefly Raza's boot heels drummed against the floor as his body convulsed in the throes of death.

"*Jefe!*" exclaimed the man who had his gun in Torn's back. "The gringo was going to kill you. That is why Raza struck him."

Santiago shrugged, indifferent. "And I forgot to thank him, didn't I?"

"But see, *jefe*. The gringo moves. He is not dead."

Relieved, Torn saw that this was so. Burton moaned, moved slightly. Still unconscious, but—thank God—still alive.

"That is not the point, Sanchez," said Santiago, his patience strained, and speaking as though he were a teacher trying to make a backward pupil understand a simple equation. "Raza did not think. He could have ruined everything. He could have killed the gringo.

And that was not the plan. This man Slaughter must live, or we came all this way for nothing. *Comprende?*"

"*Sí, jefe,*" muttered Sanchez.

Santiago turned back to Torn. "I have a message for Señor Slaughter. The only reason you live is so that you can deliver it. I am taking his daughter. Tell him no harm will come to her if he does what he is told."

"What does he have to do?"

"All in good time."

Torn's first instinct was to fight. These bastards were going to abduct Meg Slaughter, and the thought of it was almost more than he could bear. But if he made a hostile move, they would kill him. And then they would still take Meg. The only way to help her was to stay alive.

It was almost too much to ask, but he had to stand by and do nothing.

Santiago started to turn away, but a thought occurred to him, and he looked back, smiling grimly. "You want to come after the girl, hombre. It is written all over your face. But if you do, I will kill her. And I will kill you, too. But I will keep that knife, to remember you by."

Torn forced himself to meet Meg's gaze. He wanted to tell her that he *would* be coming after her. He *would* save her. But he did not speak, tried instead to let his eyes communicate the message.

"*Venga, muchachos,*" snapped Santiago.

He and the bandit restraining Meg left first. The other two backed out after them, warily keeping their guns trained on Torn. Their horses were just outside, and by the time Torn reached the door, they were gone.

He heard a smattering of gunfire across town. Pillars

of smoke from burning buildings dimmed the new sun. The smell of death lay heavy in the air.

The raid was over. Santiago had done what he had come to do.

Sunlight struck Torn full in the face, but he did not feel its heat. He was cold. Cold, clean through. He thought about Melony Hancock, abducted by Yankee deserters just days prior to his return home, following his escape from Point Lookout. He had always felt guilty about not being there when his fiancée had needed him most. To a degree, it had been that guilt which had given him the strength to search so long for Melony.

And now this. The same thing, happening all over again. A recurring nightmare.

This time, though, the outcome would be different. He was going to get Meg Slaughter back.

Or die trying.

CHAPTER 9

After Santiago's raid, Eagle Pass could have used the services of a dozen doctors. But the community boasted of only one physician and an old Mexican *curandero*—a healer—and the latter, in the opinion of most, was not much better than a witch doctor, and a long mile past crazy to boot. When all the grim and fearful accounting was done, eleven civilians had been slain, and three times that number injured.

Fortunately for Burton Slaughter, Torn knew something about wounds. He did not risk moving the injured man. Examining Slaughter's scalp, he found a deep, ugly gash. The skull was fractured, the wound bleeding profusely, as head wounds were prone to do. Burton was slipping in and out of consciousness, sometimes mumbling deliriously. Torn grabbed a duster hanging on a peg beside the back door, rolled it up, and put it under Slaughter's head. He tore strips from a linen tablecloth and applied a dressing to curtail the bleeding.

Just as he finished, someone stumbled through the back door. Edgy, Torn nearly triggered the Colt Peacemaker.

"Don't shoot, mister!" sobbed a young man clad in a soiled and tattered nightshirt. He looked to be fifteen, sixteen years old. His dusty face was streaked with tears, twisted with grief.

Torn lowered the Colt. "Relax, boy. What's your name?"

"Rand. Johnny Rand." A fresh batch of tears welled up in his eyes. "They . . . they murdered my pa. Shot him down right in front of me."

Torn laid a firm hand on Johnny Rand's bony shoulder. He said nothing; there were no words of comfort that would be of any real service to the boy. Only time could blunt the pain.

"They . . . they busted into Pa's store. We'd just got there, to do some work before opening up. Pa jumped the first one through the door, yelled at me to get out the back. Pa didn't have time to grab a gun or anything. He never much believed in guns anyhow. Just went at that Mexican with his bare fists."

"Your father's name was Ezra Rand, wasn't it?"

"Yes, sir."

Torn nodded. Rand and Burton Slaughter had been business partners, Burton providing the capital for Rand to open a general store. Coming west after the war with nothing but a pocketful of dust and a strong desire to make something out of himself, Slaughter had become a very big man in these parts. He had quite a few pokers in the fire—owned a couple of mines, operated a freighting outfit, and acted as the silent partner and money man in several Eagle Pass enterprises.

Johnny Rand was staring at Slaughter. "He ain't dead, is he, mister?"

"No. God willing, he'll pull through. He needs a doctor. I want you to stay here with him, son, while I fetch the sawbones. If he comes to, keep him still. Will you do that?"

Johnny nodded. "Where's Meg? Is Meg all right?"

Turning quickly away so that Johnny could not see the truth in his expression, Torn said, "She's alive."

It was all he could trust himself to say.

"What if . . . ?"

Torn turned back.

Johnny was trembling. "What if they come back?"

"They won't. They're halfway to the border by now."

They got what they came for.

Johnny didn't look very reassured, so Torn gave him the Peacemaker before walking outside for a firsthand look at the death and destruction Santiago's bandits had left in their wake.

The terrible sights he saw stoked a slow-burning rage down deep inside him. He gazed upon the corpses of women and children. He saw the grief and shock in the ashen faces of survivors. Half the town seemed to be on fire. The sheriff was dead, having gone down with guns blazing, witnesses said. A wounded bandit had been captured and summarily executed, hanged from a cottonwood down near Indio Wash by a passel of irate townfolk. Justice served, in Torn's opinion.

Torn had not seen anything like it since the war. It reminded him of the carnage wrought upon his home state of South Carolina by the bluecoats of Sherman's invading army. The federals had indulged in wholesale looting and pillaging. Of course, most of them had not waged war on the civilian population, but some had—those who had deserted Sherman's columns to engage in an orgy of murder and rape and theft unfettered by even a modicum of military discipline. Such men had destroyed Ravenoak, Torn's ancestral home in Clarendon County. They had taken everything of value, down to the last piece of silverware, and then destroyed the place, leaving not a single brick in place.

Sherman himself had said it: "War is hell." And as he wandered through what remained of Eagle Pass, Torn seconded the notion.

He came upon a small group of men gathered in the middle of a street. They were armed and angry. They spoke of pursuing the bandits who had dared to violate their homes. Torn listened to their hostile posturing, sized them up, and decided they could be of no help to him in what he had to do. These men were town dwellers. Their rage was genuine, but their resolve was doubtful. In a stand-up fight against the likes of Santiago's *pistoleros* they would have no chance. Those who did not flee in terror would die like dogs. Torn moved on.

Reaching the livery, he discovered that his claybank gelding had been taken by the bandits, along with just about every other cayuse in town worth throwing a saddle over.

He finally found the doctor, striving to save the life of a young woman who had been raped and then shot twice and left for dead. His arms red with blood up to the elbows, his voice hollow with emotion, the physician promised to come look at Burton Slaughter as soon as possible. Torn didn't think it would be anytime soon, but he didn't make an issue of it.

Back at Burton's house, he found his friend's condition unchanged. But a significant change had come over Johnny Rand. The youngster was sitting in a corner of the hall, knees drawn up tight against his chest, the Colt Peacemaker in both hands. He was turning the gun this way and that, examining it from every angle. There were no more tears. He was sullen, tight-lipped, his eyes bright, like those of a person consumed by fever. He didn't notice Torn until Torn was standing over him. Then he looked up slowly.

"I know who did this," he said.

"Garza Santiago."

"Not just him. Flynn put him up to it."

"Flynn?"

"Aloysius Flynn. You know."

"No, I don't."

Johnny Rand was staring at Torn as though he'd never seen him before. "They took Meg, didn't they? She ain't here, so they must've. Didn't they?"

"Yes."

Johnny nodded. It all made perfect sense to him. "Yeah, Flynn had a hand in this. I just know it. Which means he as much as killed my pa. So I'm gonna kill him if it's the last thing I do. Santiago, too."

Torn sat on his heels. "You better tell me more, son."

"You were Mr. Slaughter's friend. Didn't he tell you about Flynn?"

"No, he didn't. Why don't you?"

"I heard Pa and him talking about it a couple of times. He was Pa's partner."

"That much I do know."

"Flynn owns the Coronado Cattle Company. Biggest spread in these parts. Owns other things, too. Mines and such. Wants to own this whole town. But Mr. Slaughter stood in his way. Before the railroad came through last year, we had to bring everything in by wagon. Flynn ran the one and only freighting outfit for a while, and he was strangling us with high rates. He tried to get a lot of local businesses to let him buy in as a partner. You know, give him a percentage. That was the only way, he'd say, to get lower freight rates. Finally Mr. Slaughter said he'd had enough. So he started his own freight company.

"It got off to a rough start. No one could ever prove it, but everybody knew it was Flynn behind a passel of road agents who began to hit Mr. Slaughter's wagons. Thing about Mr. Slaughter, once he makes up his mind to do something, he'll do it, even if it harelips every cow west of the Big Muddy. So he paid hired guns to protect his wagons, and at the same time cut his rates down to nothing. Of course, just about everybody in town was doing business with him anyway. But Flynn lost a lot of money before he realized he wasn't going to stop Mr. Slaughter and went ahead and closed down his outfit."

"But there are still hard feelings between them."

Johnny nodded. "Flynn's made it plain he wants to run Mr. Slaughter out of this country."

"But how can you know that Flynn and Santiago are in cahoots?"

"I just know, is all," snapped Johnny, truculent. "They took Meg, didn't they? That's ironclad proof right there that Flynn has a hand in this. It's no mystery he hates Mr. Slaughter something fierce."

Torn realized that the feelings Johnny Rand had for Meg Slaughter were no mystery, either.

"I'm gonna go find Flynn," said Johnny, getting to his feet.

"If what you suspect is true, killing Flynn and Santiago won't bring Meg back."

"Get out of my way, mister."

"I'm Burton's friend, too."

"Then why didn't he tell you about Flynn?"

"Because Burton's always been the kind who fights

his own fights. He won't let his friends buy in because he doesn't want to see them hurt."

Shoulders bunched and chin down, Johnny Rand started to move past Torn, heading for the door.

"Listen, son . . ."

"Don't throw your shadow on me!" yelled Johnny, spinning, lifting the Colt.

Torn grabbed the Peacemaker's barrel with his left hand and pulled. Johnny lurched forward, straight into a carefully measured right hook. His knees went rubbery. His eyes rolled up in their sockets. He collapsed at Torn's feet, out cold.

Going back up to his room, Torn put on a shirt and a black frock coat. He strapped on his gun belt and the saber-knife's shoulder harness. When he went back downstairs, he took a couple of blankets with him and covered Burton with them. He knelt there a moment, his hand on Slaughter's chest, feeling the faint but steady beat of the man's heart.

"Hang on, old friend," murmured Torn. "I'll bring her back to you, safe and sound. You have my word on it."

He stood, stepped over the unconscious Johnny Rand and out into the dusty white heat of morning. Winchester racked over his shoulder, he bent his steps in the direction of Camp Warren.

CHAPTER 10

LIEUTENANT CHAPMAN EMERGED FROM THE CAMP WARREN hospital building and paused to adjust to the blinding brightness and hammering heat of the late-morning sun. Having lost a lot of blood, he was light-headed, and felt brittle, empty.

The parade ground swarmed with activity as burial details went about the business of cleaning up after the Grim Reaper. Mounted men used ropes to drag the carcasses of dead horses out of the compound. A grim silence pervaded, broken by the rasp of picks and shovels thrust into sandy soil, and the frenzied buzz of blowflies swarming around open wounds. A host of turkey buzzards circled lazily in the bleached sky.

Chapman aimed himself at the post headquarters across the way and took it one step at a time. The surgeon had said he'd been lucky; the bullet had passed clean through his shoulder, chipping but not shattering any bones. It was the loss of blood that was making him so weak and dizzy. Just staying on his feet took a monumental effort. Every time he thought he was on the verge of passing out he reminded himself of his responsibility as an officer of the United States Army. He had to maintain the dignity of the rank and uniform. By God, he had to set an example for the troopers. They were watching him as he passed, pausing in their work to whisper among themselves. Irritated, Chapman wondered what they were saying about him.

In a thin strip of purple shade on the west side of the headquarters building, three Indian scouts sat on their heels. They all wore blue cavalry tunics. One, the Tonkawa, was smoking an oak-leaf cigarette. The other two, one young, one old, were Lipan Apache. As Chapman drew near, the young Apache rose and nodded gravely at him. A corporal's stripes adorned the sleeve of his dusty tunic. In addition, he wore a broadcloth, desert moccasins, and a red headband. He carried a Spencer carbine cradled in his left arm, an army-issue revolver in a flap holster on his hip, a knife in his belt. Dark eyes in a long, bronze, inscrutable face were fastened on Chapman with the intensity of a hawk's.

His name was Codi. In Chapman's opinion, he was hands down the best damned scout the Third Cavalry possessed. Codi was very serious for one so young, and very wise. A bond of respect and trust existed between the scout and the lieutenant. Chapman felt better when Codi accompanied his patrols. The Apache could track an ant over bare rock.

For his part, Codi considered Chapman the best officer in the garrison. The lieutenant had been born and bred to this country. In some ways he knew it as well as did Codi himself. Most of the other officers were transplanted easterners. They cursed the desert and never tried to come to terms with it. And they did not respect the scouts the way Chapman did. In fact, some of them did not try to conceal their contempt for Indians. They would not listen. They thought they knew better. Chapman had an open mind. He was always willing to learn.

Chapman was pleased to see that Codi had survived the bandit attack. He understood that Codi's standing as he approached was a gesture of respect. He nodded gratefully, and walked on. No words passed between them. They seemed to be able to communicate a great deal without speaking.

Inside post headquarters, Chapman told the orderly he wished to see Colonel Dalworth.

"Yes, sir, Lieutenant. In fact, he just ordered me to send someone after you."

Chapman passed through into Dalworth's office.

The colonel sat behind his desk. A tall, lean man dressed in black stood before it. Dalworth was hunched forward, posture and expression similar to those of a man suffering from a severe bellyache. Chapman could guess what was ailing Dalworth. This morning's disaster was tailor-made for career busting.

"Lieutenant, I am relieved to see you up and about," said Dalworth. "I heard you had been wounded. I was also informed that you conducted yourself in an exemplary fashion during the attack. I assure you that will figure in my report."

Dalworth winced at the thought of making that particular report.

"Thank you, sir," said Chapman. Was that, then, what the men had been discussing as they watched him cross the parade ground? How well he had done in the fight? He couldn't remember much about it, except being scared right down to his socks.

"I sent for you. . ." began Dalworth.

"Colonel, I've come to request permission to leave the camp."

"For what purpose?"

"I have to go into town, sir."

"I've already sent details to help fight fires and assist in every other way possible."

"This is personal business, Colonel." Chapman faltered, but plunged on. "I want to make sure Meg Slaughter is well."

Dalworth glanced sharply at the man in black. "Lieutenant, let me introduce Mr. Clay Torn. A federal judge, and a friend of Burton Slaughter's. Mr. Slaughter was seriously wounded this morning. Judge Torn, Lieutenant Chapman."

"I'd been told Mr. Slaughter had a houseguest," said Chapman.

"Meg is alive, Lieutenant," said Torn. "But you won't find her in Eagle Pass. Santiago took her hostage."

Chapman paled. The room tilted. He closed his eyes tightly, braced himself against the desk.

"Are you all right, Lieutenant?" asked Dalworth, alarmed.

Somehow Chapman pulled himself together. "Just a little light-headed, sir. Loss of blood."

"Judge Torn has just told me a fantastic story," said Dalworth. "I sent for you because I want you to hear it. I am a relative newcomer to this area; you grew up in these parts. You would know better than I whether any credence should be lent to what he says. Judge?"

Torn repeated to Chapman what he had just finished telling Dalworth: a concise, unembellished rendering of Johnny Rand's theory regarding Burton Slaughter, Aloysius Flynn, and Garza Santiago.

Chapman could scarcely concentrate on what Torn was saying. All he could think about was Meg's plight.

When Torn was done, Chapman was too preoccupied to make a comment.

Dalworth leaped into the breach of Chapman's silence. "I cannot bring myself to believe it. The Rand boy is crazy with grief. For one thing, Flynn owns the Coronado Cattle Company, and we received word only hours before the attack that the Coronado foreman and several vaqueros were ambushed and killed by Santiago's men."

Chapman glared at Dalworth and almost lost his temper. He teetered on the brink of cursing his commanding officer for being a fool. If the man had not been such an incompetent—if he had taken the vaquero's warning seriously—the raid might not have occurred.

And Meg would be safe and sound at this moment.

It was an act of insubordination that he was contemplating, and it would cost him his commission—could even result in court-martial. But he didn't care about that. His career seemed supremely unimportant at the moment. It was the fact that he didn't want to give Dalworth the satisfaction that held him in check.

"Where is the man who brought word of this to you?" Torn asked Dalworth. "I want to talk to him."

The colonel grimaced. "He vanished during the raid. We can't find a trace of him. My point, however, is that were Santiago and Flynn conspiring together, Santiago would not have killed Flynn's hired hands."

Torn pondered that a moment. "If it really happened."

"I believe it did," insisted Dalworth.

In his agitated state, Chapman couldn't hold back any longer. Dalworth believed it now, but he hadn't a few hours ago! The lieutenant opened his mouth to make a sarcastic point about this inconsistency—but Torn beat him to it—for the moment, at least, saving one shavetail's career.

"Then why didn't you act on the information, Colonel?"

Dalworth turned beet red. "I don't have to answer to you, sir!"

Torn was not intimidated by this high-ranking officer's bluster. He leaned over the desk, his gray eyes cold and sharp, like tempered steel. "What are you going to do about it now?"

Dalworth sat rigid, fists clenched, and tried to stare Torn down.

He failed.

"My hands are tied," he mumbled, lowering his gaze. "Santiago ran off most of our mounts. And even if we were in any condition to pursue, the fact remains we cannot cross the border in force."

"So Mexican bandits can come over here, burn our towns, kill our citizens, and nothing will be done to balance the scales?"

"I've wired district headquarters. Even as we speak, news of the raid is on its way to Washington. I can only wait for orders. But I am sure those orders will not include violating the sovereignty of the Republic of Mexico."

Torn was equally sure. He knew exactly what would happen. Diplomats would take over. There would be a lot of talk, but in the end, good relations between the two governments would take priority over avenging the wrong done to a small Texas town.

And Dalworth? He could only wait—for the ax to fall. The colonel was going to play the role of scapegoat. The man's career was ruined. Torn's anger subsided, replaced by pity.

"Maybe you have to wait," he said. "But I don't."

"I remind you, sir, that you are a federal judge. A government official. You can't—"

"Yes, I can. I just resigned."

Dalworth jumped up as Torn spun on his heel and made for the door. "I can't allow you to—"

"Try to stop me, Colonel," said Torn, in a low-down whisper, "and you'll have another fight on your hands."

CHAPTER 11

As soon as Torn was gone, Dalworth denied Lieutenant Chapman permission to leave Camp Warren. He gave no reason. He didn't have to.

Seething with anger, Chapman returned to his quarters. The only motive he could assign to the colonel's refusal was pure spite. Dalworth could see how much he wanted to go into Eagle Pass. It didn't matter that Meg Slaughter wasn't there. He just had to do something, even if what he did failed to accomplish anything. He couldn't just sit here idle; he was edgy with despair.

He tried to sleep. Although he was exhausted, sleep eluded him. He got up and paced the floor. He stepped outside, but the sight of the carnage wrought a few hours before depressed him even more. Back inside, he paced some more. His pulse was racing. His face felt hot. The wound in his shoulder made walking painful, but that pain was nothing compared with the unbearable agony twisting his soul.

Meg. In the hands of Santiago's bastards.

After an hour of restless pacing his knees buckled and he had to sit down on the edge of the bed. He put his head in his hands. He tried to force himself to calm down. Think. Repress the emotions boiling inside him.

But all he could think about was Meg. Wonderful, beautiful Meg, suffering God only knew what . . .

No. He had to stop thinking such thoughts. He was going to drive himself to madness.

Though born in the *brasada,* a mustanger's son, Chapman had been fortunate to have a mother who believed the ability to read and write were important. With these rudiments, and the sponsorship of an army officer who had been a close friend of his father's, Chapman had been accepted to West Point. He had done well at the academy. He had learned to look at a problem from all angles to find the solution, and to do so calmly under tremendous pressure. These lessons he tried to apply to his present situation. He tried to remove himself from the problem and look at it with the objectivity of an outsider.

In doing this, he came to reconsider his opinion of Colonel Dalworth. The colonel had seen right through him, knowing what he was on the verge of doing before he'd realized the truth himself. Dalworth wasn't a complete fool after all.

He'd seen it in Chapman's eyes, heard it in his voice. And now, standing on the outside looking in, Chapman saw it, too.

He was going after Santiago to rescue Meg, and he didn't give a tinker's damn if it took him into Mexico, or even through the gates of hell.

It meant desertion. Court-martial was a certainty if

he were caught; execution a distinct possibility. At the very least he would serve a very long prison sentence. He weighed these consequences against his feelings for Meg. It was no contest. Love won out.

What did his career matter without Meg? Somehow he had always known he and Meg were meant for each other. Other men courted her, but Chapman had never wavered in his conviction that she would be his wife. He couldn't imagine living without her.

"I'll do it," he muttered to the four adobe walls. "I have to."

He shot to his feet. Two long strides carried him across the room, and he threw open the door.

Codi was standing there.

The Apache studied Chapman's face, recognized the determined set of the lieutenant's jaw, the wild gleam in his eye.

Chapman realized the scout knew exactly what he intended to do.

"I go with you," said Codi.

Chapman was thunderstruck. Gratitude welled up inside him. The prospect of having Codi along gave him a glimmer of honest hope. Not for himself. For Meg. Because Chapman knew he didn't stand a chance of getting the job done alone.

Codi hated Mexicans—it had something to do with his family. Chapman didn't know all the details; Codi kept his hurt very private. Yet the lieutenant sensed it was friendship rather than hatred that was prompting Codi to throw in with him.

Shunned by his own people for helping the "yellow-legs," the cavalry was all Codi had. He was immensely proud of the uniform he wore, with its two corporal's stripes. But he was willing now to throw all that away, and put his life on the line in the bargain, to help Chapman.

The Apache was a true friend. But as much as he wanted Codi's help, Chapman couldn't accept such sacrifice.

"I can't let you do it," he said.

Codi was inscrutable. "I go."

"I order you to stay."

Codi frowned.

"You've never disobeyed an order before," said Chapman, pressing his advantage. Honor and duty were everything to the scout.

Codi was shrewd, and he spent only a moment thinking his way around the obstacle Chapman had thrown in his path.

The ghost of a smile haunted the corner of his mouth. "You deserter. No more lieutenant. Just friend now. I go."

Chapman started to protest, then realized it was futile. Codi had made up his mind. If he said he was going to do something, it was good as done.

"We'll need a couple of fast horses with a lot of 'bottom,'" said Chapman.

"You wait, Indio Wash. I get horses."

Codi held up three fingers as he spoke the last word.

"Why three?"

"Man in black. He go."

"How do you know?"

Codi shrugged. "I see. I hear. I know."

Chapman nodded wryly. "Three horses, then."

The scout turned and walked away.

Closing the door, Chapman quickly loaded all the ammunition he had into saddlebags. He gazed ruefully at the "U.S." branded into the worn brown leather of the pannier flaps. Rifling the contents of a small trunk at the foot of the bed, he found a small pouch. Inside were his life's savings. Almost two hundred dollars. He had been saving it for his marriage to Meg. He had wanted to be able to give her everything her heart desired. The fact that her father was one of the richest men in the area didn't enter into his calculations. A man had to provide for his wife and family on his own.

Now, though, he would have to spend it to rescue Meg. First, he'd have to purchase civilian clothes. He couldn't very well traipse through Mexico on Garza Santiago's trail wearing army blue.

He paused a moment, staring blankly at the wall, glimpsing the future. What kind of life could a deserter offer the woman he loved?

Because the minute he stepped out that door, he would be on the run for the rest of his life.

Despondent, he found his thoughts turning to Clay Torn. Another man willing to sacrifice his career to rescue Meg. Or was it because Burton Slaughter was his friend. Surely it had nothing to do with Meg. It couldn't. Torn had been here only a handful of days.

Still, jealousy stabbed Chapman in the heart.

At that moment young Oliver Chapman began to think of Torn as more a rival than an ally.

CHAPTER 12

SANTIAGO'S MEN HAD ABSCONDED WITH MOST OF CAMP Warren's horses; Dalworth didn't have enough to mount a troop. The soldiers he dispatched to Eagle Pass for the purpose of assisting the citizenry and maintaining law and order in the wake of the local sheriff's death had to be transported in Dougherty wagons. Torn caught a ride back to town on one of these.

The troopers were curious about him, but they left him alone. He did not look to be in the best of moods. He brooded over the discovery that the army was powerless to do anything about Garza Santiago. In retrospect, he wasn't really too surprised. And it didn't shake his resolve; he knew what he had to do. His chances of rescuing Meg alone were virtually nil, but he had to try.

Back at Burton Slaughter's house, he found that the doctor had finally arrived. Johnny Rand was still there.

He had helped the physician move Burton to a cowhide sofa in the parlor, beneath the portrait of his wife.

"He's conscious now," the doctor informed Torn as they stood in the downstairs hall. The sawbones seemed to have aged ten years since dawn.

"Will he pull through?"

The doctor's shrug was noncommittal. "Head injuries are a tricky business. Hard to say. But he's strong as an ox. One thing is certain: he must have complete rest. He's . . . he's asking after his daughter." The physician glanced across at Johnny, who stood a little apart from them. "I'm told she was taken."

Torn grimaced. "Did you tell Burton?"

"No. I . . . I don't know. I was afraid the shock might kill him."

"Not knowing will kill him. He'll assume the worst."

"What could be worse?"

"She could be dead."

"She might be better off."

"Long as you draw breath," snapped Torn, irritated, "you've got a chance."

The doctor nodded. "I've got more work to do. I'll drop by later to check on him." He gave Torn a long, bleak look. "I don't envy you."

Torn knew what the doctor meant by that. It was up to him to break the news to Burton.

Slaughter held up surprisingly well. He tried to get up, but Torn put a hand on his shoulder and gently pushed him down again.

"Don't worry," said Torn. "I'll bring your daughter back to you."

Burton squeezed his eyes tightly shut. But he didn't crack. "She's all I have, Clay," he whispered. "The only thing that makes it worth a damn. Everything I've done, I did for her. Everything I built . . ."

"I know."

"Why? Why did they take her?"

"It was Garza Santiago."

"My God."

"Have you crossed his path before?"

"No. Never."

"He said no harm would come to her if you did as you were told."

"I'll do anything. What is it? Money? They can have it all. What do I have to do?"

"I expect you'll find out very soon."

"If he harms a hair on her head, I'll kill the bastard. I'll kill him slow."

"Why didn't you tell me about Aloysius Flynn?"

Slaughter was startled. "What's Flynn got to do with this? Wait a minute. You don't think Flynn and Santiago are . . . ?"

Torn shrugged. "What do you think?"

Slaughter stared off into space.

"Flynn wants to be the big augur in these parts. Wants to run everything. I stand in his way. Frankly I wouldn't put anything past him. Clay . . ." Burton grabbed Torn's arm. For a man in such a weakened condition, his grip was surprisingly strong. "Clay, can you save her?"

"I won't come back without her."

Returning to the hall, he looked for Johnny Rand, having made up his mind to ask the boy to look after Burton. But Johnny had vanished. Torn heard horses out behind the house. His Winchester leaned against the wall beside the door to the front parlor. He snatched it up on his way to the back door.

It was Lieutenant Chapman and one of the scouts Torn recalled seeing near Camp Warren's headquarters' building. The Indian was leading a third horse.

"You ready?" asked Chapman.

Torn noticed the bulge of bandages under Chapman's tunic. The lieutenant's features were drawn with pain.

"You don't look fit for a long trail, Lieutenant."

"Don't worry about me."

"What's your stake in this?"

"Meg Slaughter."

Torn's smile was bleak. There was an underlying challenge in Chapman's answer. "I guess you resigned, too," he said dryly.

"In a manner of speaking." Chapman was brusque. "We're going after Santiago. So are you. We might as well stick together. Unless you're suddenly back to being a federal judge, and you're too good to ride with a deserter."

Torn's steel-cast eyes swung to the horse the Indian scout was leading. He saw the "U.S." brand on its flank. The horse was stolen property, and once he got aboard, he was asking to get his neck stretched.

But why worry about that? Odds were good he wouldn't get out of Mexico alive.

"You two will have to get shed of those army blues," he said, striding to the extra mount. He took the reins from Codi and stepped into the saddle.

"Later," said Chapman. "Right now they serve a purpose. Troopers we run into around here will assume we're away from the post on orders."

Torn wondered how long it would take Colonel Dalworth to realize Chapman and the scout were gone. The post was in disarray after the raid; that fact might buy them a few hours.

"Let's get going," said Chapman. He remembered something his father had always said when rousting his mustanger crew out of their soogans at the crack of dawn. "We're burning daylight."

"We've got one stop to make before we cross the border," said Torn. "You know where to find Aloysius Flynn?"

"His place is down by the river. But what makes you think he'll tell you anything even if he is involved?"

Torn shrugged. "We need to know what we're up against."

CHAPTER 13

ALOYSIUS FLYNN OWNED PROPERTY ON BOTH SIDES OF THE Rio Grande. The Mexican portion of his cattle empire he had acquired by marriage. His wife, now deceased, had been the only child of Don Tomas Chagres de Obregón. Fifty thousand acres of Coahuila *brasada* had been her dowry. All of this Flynn had inherited.

Some said Mrs. Flynn's riding accident hadn't been an accident at all, but they didn't speak too loudly, because Flynn was a very powerful—as well as a very unforgiving—man.

He had influence in Mexico City. His interests south of the border remained largely untouched by the turmoil that seemed to be forever racking that country; one of the reasons was his generous and ongoing contribution to the personal coffers of Porfirio Díaz.

Flynn and Díaz weren't friends. It was a purely business arrangement. In fact, Flynn had been just as generous with Porfirio's predecessor. And he was ready to make the same arrangement with the man who replaced Díaz. In Mexico, heads of state usually didn't last much longer than a cowboy's paycheck.

Nobody could say for sure how many longhorns roamed Flynn's spread, but the Coronado Cattle Company employed over a hundred top hands, most of them vaqueros. Still, being a certified cattle baron wasn't enough for Flynn. He'd come over from Ireland a scrawny, barefoot kid without a plug nickel to his name, and such destitute beginnings had something to do with the way he was now, and the way he always would be: hungry for money, and the power money could buy.

All this Chapman told Torn as they rode through the sun-blistered malpais. The lieutenant knew plenty about Flynn.

"My father crossed swords with him a few times," said Chapman. "Flynn thought that every mustang found on his range belonged to him. My father thought otherwise. There could have been some bloodshed, except that Flynn finally backed down. My father's mustangers were a pretty wild bunch. Flynn's cowboys were no match for them."

Torn was beginning to form a mental picture of Aloysius Flynn as a man who lacked the backbone to stand firm when push came to shove. But Flynn had money, so he didn't need courage. He could buy plenty of brave men to do his dirty work for him.

Late in the afternoon they topped a hogback ridge and sat their horses a moment to gaze down into the valley of the Rio Grande. The river was a thin blue snake twisting through groves of dusty gray cottonwoods and pale green willows. Directly below them was Flynn's hacienda. Chapman's sense of direction had been unerring. He had led them right to the spot, and

Torn considered himself fortunate to be riding with men who knew their way in this country.

Flynn's house was built like a fortress, a two-story affair surrounding a courtyard. Chapman had brought a pair of Vollmer field glasses, and he let Torn use them to get a better look. The walls of the house were adobe, impervious to bullets, arrows, and fire. The windows were tall and narrow, the doors made with heavy beams reinforced with strap iron. The roof was flat, and the outer walls rose above the roof line to form a parapet. Torn spotted two men with rifles posted as lookouts on the roof.

"Looks like Flynn's expecting trouble," he said. "He's got sentries on the roof."

"Common practice," replied Chapman. "They call this the Bloody Border for a reason. Bandits, renegade Comanches—name your poison, and you'll find it down here."

Torn was silent a moment, peering through the field glasses, paying careful attention to detail. In addition to the hacienda, there were corrals and breaking pens, three bunkhouses, a smokehouse, and smithy. West of the big house were two dozen smaller dwellings, the *ranchito* where the vaqueros who were married lived with their families. Some men were breaking horses, a woman was hanging out the wash. Normal activity. But one thing seemed out of the ordinary.

"Pretty quiet," remarked Chapman.

Lowering the field glasses, Torn gave him a long look. "You don't think there's much chance Flynn and Santiago are in cahoots, do you?"

"I do not. Flynn's not much of a gambler, and he has too much to lose to put his money on the wrong horse. No, he'd go with the sure bet, and right now that's Díaz.

As far as the so-called revolutionaries are concerned, he's just another filthy rich *haciendero*."

"Maybe," said Torn. "Maybe not."

"One thing you can't get around. Santiago killed four of Flynn's men."

"I'd like to talk to the man who brought you that news."

"Well, let's go down and see if he's here," said Chapman, impatient. "Then maybe we can get on with the business of finding Meg."

"Two things," said Torn. "First, since you're still wearing that uniform, you'll tell Flynn that Colonel Dalworth sent you to find the vaquero who warned you about Santiago's coming. Second, make no mention of Meg Slaughter's abduction."

"I hope you know what you're doing, because I don't. And how do I explain you, by the way?"

"I'll take care of that." Torn glanced at Codi. "I want you to wait here until dark. Then I want to know why there's a guard posted at the smokehouse."

He handed Codi the field glasses.

The Apache's sharp eyes had already spotted the man to whom Torn referred, but he used the field glasses to get a closer look. The guard was leaning against the stone wall of the smokehouse, his sombrero pulled low against the slanting sun. Cigarette smoke trickled out from under the brim. He had a repeating rifle cradled in his arms.

"Why would there be a guard at the smokehouse?" Chapman wondered aloud.

"Something in there more valuable than a side of beef," surmised Torn.

"Anh," said Codi. "Yes. I will find out."

"Don't kill the guard if you can help it," said Torn.

"We don't know yet if those folks down there are our enemies."

Codi nodded. "No kill."

"Let's ride, Lieutenant," said Torn.

They headed down into the valley, stirrup to stirrup, as the long purple shadows of evening reached across the malpais.

CHAPTER 14

THE LOOKOUTS ON THE ROOF OF FLYNN'S HACIENDA spotted their dust before they had gone very far down the slope, and the call rang out across the valley, through the still twilight.

"Riders coming!"

Men and women emerged from the *chozas*—huts—in the *ranchito,* and more men emerged curiously from the bunkhouses. In the half-light of dusk none of them could tell much of anything about Torn and Chapman at first, but as the distance diminished, the lieutenant's uniform was recognized. Torn saw one of the vaqueros hasten into the hacienda. A woman was lighting storm lanterns along the sweeping gallery, and it was by the warm yellow light of these that Torn had his first look at Aloysius Flynn.

The man who emerged through the big double doors of iron-braced mountain mahogany was clearly the ruler of this roost. He stood with feet planted well apart and hands on hips—the posture of a man who is lord of all he surveys. He was a short man, yet managed to appear as though he were looking down on all others. Here, thought Torn, was an ambitious man, one for whom the end would justify the means.

Flynn made up in brawn what he lacked in stature. He was built low and wide. A thick sandy beard covered his face. His gimlet eyes, deep set beneath a jutting brow, were shamrock green. The backs of his ham-sized hands were thick with hair the color of rust. He wore a plain white shirt, durable twill trousers, and hand-tooled boots. A pearl-handled revolver was stuck under a broad leather belt.

Now that it was evident that the two riders were not just a couple of cowboys coming in off the range, a crowd began to gather in front of the hacienda. Torn and Chapman checked their lathered horses in front of the big house and found themselves surrounded by half a hundred people. Torn sized the men up as tough, wiry *brasaderos,* every one. Men who knew their way around guns but didn't make a living with them. Therein lay the subtle difference between them and Torn; most of them would think twice before killing a fellow human being. Torn would do it without blinking an eye. It was an attribute he wasn't particularly proud of, but he knew it to be the key to his survival in a life of violence.

"Mr. Flynn," said Chapman. "I'm Lieutenant—"

"I know who you are." Flynn's gravelly voice crackled like heat lightning. A trace of an Irish brogue still lingered in it. His tone was crisp, but not uncivil. "Step down, Lieutenant. By the look of your pony, you've come a long way in a short time. What brings you in such a hurry?"

"There's been some trouble." Chapman swung down out of the saddle, stiff from long hours of hard riding. "This morning, Garza Santiago and his bandits attacked Camp Warren and raided Eagle Pass."

Torn watched Flynn closely as a murmur of surprise rippled through the crowd. Impassive, Flynn rocked slightly on the balls of his feet. When he spoke, the crowd fell silent.

"Santiago has nerve, I'll give him that. Much damage done?"

"They burned about half the town."

Flynn nodded. "What folks get when they build their homes out of sticks instead of mud. You can't beat adobe. It turns back arrows and bullets and laughs at fire. Casualties?"

"Some. But Santiago paid dearly."

"Well, in his world, life is cheap. He paid nothing he couldn't easily afford. Lot of men south of the river who are willing to trade old age for a few years of living without rules and just taking whatever tickles their fancy."

"You don't seem too surprised," remarked Torn.

Flynn fastened his flinty gaze on Torn and said, "You're welcome, too, stranger. Step down and lighten that pony's load."

Torn dismounted. To address someone who was afoot while remaining in the saddle was a breach of frontier etiquette.

"I'm not surprised, frankly," continued Flynn. "Our towns over here are fat pigs ready for slaughter. The only thing surprises me is that Santiago, or one of the many others like him, haven't ventured across the river before now. I'll wager they flamin' well cleaned out Eagle Pass. Stripped the shebangs down to the bare bones. Hit the bank as well, no doubt."

Chapman glanced at Torn, brows raised in silent query. Torn shook his head. He did not know what fate had befallen the Eagle Pass bank.

"You men come on in," said Flynn. "I'll pour you something to cut the dust."

They followed Flynn into a short, wide hallway with a floor of glazed sandstone tiles, through a set of doors into a long room containing handsome old pieces of oak furniture. Mexican rugs adorned the floor. A framed map of Flynn's private empire hung above the mantel of a cold black hearth.

"Name your poison," said Flynn, making for a sideboard.

"Anything," replied Chapman, "as long as it kicks."

"Bourbon," said Torn, "if you've got it."

"A gentleman's drink," commented Flynn. "I've got everything from Madeira to mescal."

"One of your men arrived at Camp Warren before dawn," said Chapman as Flynn poured the drinks. "He said Santiago had ambushed him, Frank Robles, and three other vaqueros. Said the bandits hanged Frank and the others. He managed to escape. He must have pulled the same trick when Santiago struck the camp, because we couldn't find him after the raid. We thought he might have come here."

Flynn brought them their tongue oil. "That would be Alvarez. What he told you is true. Frank's horse wandered in here about noon. I sent some men out to backtrack it. They brought the bodies in a couple of hours ago. Got them laid out in the other room. We'll give them a decent Christian burial in the morning. As for Alvarez . . ." Flynn shrugged. "They didn't find his body, so I've been curious as to what had become of him."

Again Chapman glanced at Torn. He didn't know

what else to say. In fact, he wasn't even sure why they were wasting their time here in the first place when they needed to be hot on Santiago's trail.

"The army will have an inquiry," said Torn, deftly picking up the slack. "They'll want testimony from this man Alvarez."

"Yes, so they can crucify Dalworth. You haven't told me yet who you are, stranger."

"Torn. Clay Torn. I'm a federal judge."

"You're not from these parts."

"No."

Flynn waited, expecting elaboration, but Torn left it at that, and Flynn finally said, "If Alvarez went running to Camp Warren instead of here, he must have known Santiago was going to raid Eagle Pass." His gaze flicked to Chapman. "I would've thought you boys'd be ready for him. What happened?"

Chapman's face darkened with anger. He didn't feel like making excuses for Colonel Dalworth.

Flynn smiled. "Don't mean to put your feet in the fire, Lieutenant. I can guess what happened. Dalworth belongs back east—a civilized post. He likes to tell everybody he's a veteran of the war, but I happen to know for a fact he never got within a hundred miles of the front lines. He's not cut out to be the commandant of an army post in this kind of country. Bandits and Indians don't play by the rules."

Torn finished off the bourbon. "Mind if I have another?" he asked, turning toward the sideboard.

"Help yourself."

Torn had noted a window near the sideboard, through which he thought he could get a look at the smokehouse, thirty yards west of the hacienda.

"Why do you think Santiago killed your men?" Chapman asked Flynn.

"Why not? Santiago's kind would kill you for your spurs, Lieutenant. My guess is they hanged Frank and the others instead of shooting them because it made for better sport. The flamin' bastards."

Pouring his drink, Torn glanced out the window. It was slap dark outside now. He could make out only the vague outline of the smokehouse—could see nothing of the guard he had spotted through the field glasses. Had Codi made his move? All Torn's hopes hinged on the Apache finding some clue inside the smokehouse to confirm that Flynn was in league with Santiago. A pretty slender thread, admittedly. One you couldn't hang a whole lot of hope on. But Torn didn't have a whole lot of hope. He had a nagging suspicion that Chapman was right—that they were wasting their time here. And all the while Santiago's trail got colder. Maybe he'd been a fool for giving any credence at all to Johnny Rand's story. Every minute they tarried here put more ground between them and Meg Slaughter.

"Well," said Chapman, "we'd better be going."

"You're both welcome to stay the night," offered Flynn. "Lieutenant, you grew up out here. You should know better than to travel in this country after nightfall."

"It's an early moon," said Chapman lamely.

"What's your hurry? Santiago's clear across the border by now, so you horse soldiers can't do anything about him anyway."

"I was instructed to return to the post with all possible haste," lied Chapman, and the untruth was sour on his tongue. "You about ready, Judge? Thanks for the drink, Mr. Flynn."

He turned on his heel and made for the doors with long, impatient strides, his spurs ringing against the floor.

"The boy's got a burr under his saddle," said Flynn after Chapman had left the room. "Probably because his father and I had some differences a few years back."

Torn left his glass on the sideboard, crossed the room to shake Flynn's hand. "Thanks for the dust cutter."

"Anytime, Judge. My door's always open."

Torn went outside. Chapman was already mounted. Out in the malpais a coyote wailed, and from somewhere in the *ranchito* a dog barked in response. The crowd had dispersed. Someone in one of the bunkhouses was strumming a guitar. Down near the river, bullfrogs sang a vibrant chorus. As Torn mounted up, Flynn came out onto the gallery to watch them go.

They held their horses to a walk, riding stirrup to stirrup. Chapman waited until they were well out of earshot; he could wait no longer than that without boiling over.

"Are you satisfied?" he rasped. "We'll lose half a day trying to cut Santiago's trail. We could have followed it straight out of Camp Warren, but you had to come here. What were you hoping to find?"

"You don't have to ride with me," snapped Torn.

"By God, you're right about that at least."

A curtain of hostile silence fell between them as they rode back up the long slope to the rise from which they had first seen Flynn's hacienda.

Codi was waiting for them, right at the spot where they had parted company an hour before. The Apache was sitting on his heels, his horse ground-hitched behind him.

"Did you get in?" asked Torn.

The scout nodded.

"I hope to God you didn't kill the vaquero," said Chapman.

"No kill." Codi tapped the side of his head, behind the ear, with his fist.

"Did you find anything?" pressed Torn.

"What could he find?" asked Chapman. "We were wasting our time here, Torn, and you damn well know it. Did you expect Flynn to say something that would implicate him? Even if he was involved, he's not stupid enough—"

"Anh," said Codi. "I find something. Wait."

The scout rose, slipped into a clump of scrub cedar and returned a moment later with the vaquero named Alvarez in tow.

The Mexican's hands were tied behind his back with strips of rawhide.

"My God!" exclaimed Chapman, flabbergasted. "You!"

"Alvarez, I presume," said Torn wryly.

CHAPTER 15

"You have saved my life," declared Alvarez. "I am in your debt. So I will tell you everything you want to know."

"Not here and now," said Torn, looking over his shoulder. He could see the lights in the windows of the buildings down below. And he didn't have to hear the vaquero's story to know that Alvarez would implicate Flynn. Flynn had lied; he'd said he hadn't seen Alvarez when in fact Alvarez had obviously been his prisoner.

"That is a good idea," Alvarez concurred. "When Señor Flynn finds out I am gone, he will send many men after us. He will try to kill us all because of what I know and what you will know, once I tell you."

"Why is he tied up?" Torn asked Codi.

"He try run away," replied the scout.

Alvarez was sheepish. *"Es verdad.* I was afraid." He

glanced warily at Codi, and Torn could see he was still afraid.

"Untie him," said Torn. "As for you, Alvarez, if you try to run away again, you'll wind up coyote bait. *Comprende?*"

Alvarez nodded. He cringed as Codi drew his knife from its sheath. The scout sliced the rawhide thongs. Rubbing his wrists, the vaquero laughed nervously.

"I recognize this one. I have heard of him. He hates my people."

"He has good reason," said Chapman, rising quickly to Codi's defense. Turning to Torn, he observed, "We're short a horse."

"He take mine," suggested Codi. "I run."

Chapman nodded. It was a sensible arrangement. Like most Apache warriors, Codi possessed the lungs and legs to run for hours without respite.

As they rode away, Codi loping alongside Chapman's horse, Torn wondered how long it would be before Flynn found out Alvarez had escaped. And then how would he react?

In the past, Flynn had backed down when things got too hot to handle. He had backed down from Slaughter, and from Chapman's father. But this time Aloysius Flynn had gone too far to back down. He had too much blood on his hands. Torn didn't doubt that Alvarez had evidence linking Flynn with Santiago's raid. Johnny Rand had been right all along.

And to save his own life, Flynn would have to make dead certain that Torn, Chapman, Alvarez, and the Apache scout lost theirs.

Following the river, they put five miles behind them before stopping for the night in a brush-choked draw nestled between the shoulders of a horseshoe hill.

Codi climbed to the rim to watch their back trail. The moon had reached its zenith and was beginning its decline to the western skyline. The malpais was bathed in its silver radiance. Torn knew that capable trackers would have no difficulty following their sign as long as the moon was up. So far, though, there was no indication of pursuit.

The horses were worn to a frazzle. They were given a little water. The draw provided a little graze, clumps of mesquite grass and tanglehead. The cinches were loosened, but the saddles stayed on their backs.

Alvarez asked if he could smoke, and Torn gave the go-ahead. The vaquero built a roll-your-own. His hands shook.

"Tell me what you know," said Torn. "Is Flynn in this with Garza Santiago?"

Alvarez pushed his sombrero back from his brow and tried to smile, an effort to show Torn and Chapman that he wasn't scared to death. The attempt failed; the smile looked more like a grimace.

"*Sí*. When Santiago captured me and my *compañeros* south of the river, I overheard one of his men say we were right where we were supposed to be. At first I did not understand what he meant." Alvarez shrugged. "I was too frightened to think about it then. They were talking among themselves about the best way to kill us. All I could think about was getting away. I was lucky. They spent a lot of time trying to find me. But it was dark, and I hid in the brush until they gave up."

"Why didn't you say something about that to me or Colonel Dalworth?" asked Chapman.

"Because by then I understood. You see, Santiago knew where to look for us. And it was Señor Flynn who told Frank Robles to work that area. It was night, we had built a fire, we weren't worried about anything.

Santiago could have circled wide if he had not wanted us to know of his presence. Instead he rides straight into our camp. Why? To kill us. Señor Flynn must have told him to."

Torn nodded. "Makes sense. In a way it made Flynn a victim, too."

"That's cold-blooded murder," breathed Chapman.

"So why did you go back to Flynn if you knew this?" Torn asked Alvarez.

The vaquero sighed, looked away. "Because I am a fool. I did not tell you, *teniente,* because I thought I could make Flynn buy my silence. I saw a chance to get rich."

"Blackmail?" Torn shook his head in amazement. "What made you think Flynn wouldn't kill you on the spot?"

"I slipped into the hacienda without being seen. I knew he kept a lot of money there. I held him at gunpoint. Told him I would ride away and say nothing to anyone if he paid me to keep my mouth shut. If he didn't, I would tell the army what I knew."

"But Flynn didn't buy into that."

"No."

"Because he knew that even if you carried out your threat, no one would believe such a story."

"As I said, I was a fool."

"So how did he get the best of you?"

"He tricked me," said Alvarez, bitter. "He has a safe hidden beneath the floor. There was a gun in it. He gave me the money first, a sack of gold double eagles." The vaquero's eyes gleamed. "More money than I could make in a dozen lifetimes, hombre. And as I reached for the money he hit me. Knocked me down. When I looked up, he had the gun aimed here." Alvarez touched the bridge of his nose with a forefinger.

"I'm surprised he didn't kill you right then and there," said Torn.

"I have friends at the rancho. He told the men I had run away while Frank Robles and the others fought for their lives against Santiago. Some of the men wanted to hang me. But he said no. I would get a fair trial. It would all be—how do you say it?—fair and square. He locked me in the smokehouse, under guard. No one was to talk to me. He said it was for my own protection."

"The man's a clever bastard," said Torn. "By pretending to protect you, he cut the legs right out from under any claim you might make. None of the other men would have believed you."

"I do not think I would have seen another day. I had made my peace with God." The vaquero's voice was pitched low, and none too steady. There was a haunted look in his eyes—the eyes, mused Torn, of a man who had stared death in the face.

"So you were right about Flynn after all, Judge," admitted Chapman. "Now we know. But what good does it do us? We're on the dodge. Who'd believe us over Flynn? And this doesn't get us any closer to Santiago. Or Meg."

"But at least I know now Santiago meant it when he said no harm would come to Meg. Burton won't do what Flynn wants until he's sure his daughter is unharmed. Question is: What does Flynn want in exchange for Meg's safe return?"

Chapman thought it over. "My guess is he wants Burton Slaughter out altogether. Flynn would like to be the only bull in this pasture, and as long as Slaughter is around, he can't have it all." Agitated, Chapman began to pace. "You know, Flynn's going to figure Alvarez here has told us everything. So now he's got to kill us all. And he'll probably send a rider to warn Santiago."

"I doubt that. What does Santiago care? He doesn't work on a handshake; I reckon he's already been paid off. And why would he worry? He knows the army can't touch him now."

"No, the army can't touch him," said Chapman. "And how do we get to him? We have to go through a hundred *bandoleros* to do it. Got any more bright ideas, Judge?"

"Get your spurs out of me, Chapman."

"You know, Torn, it occurs to me that you shouldn't even be here today."

"What do you mean?"

"You were there when they took Meg. You should have at least tried to stop them. I would have. They'd have taken her over my dead body."

"Which would have done Meg a lot of good."

Chapman walked away in a huff. Torn watched him go with sympathetic eyes. He couldn't blame the lieutenant for being so edgy. This was Meg Slaughter's first night as Santiago's captive, and Chapman's imagination was giving him hell. It was going to be a long, sleepless, agonizing stretch till daybreak for the young lieutenant.

Alvarez sat on a rock, despondent. He took one last long drag on his cigarette before flicking it away. As the reddish-orange tip of the quirly flared it cast a dim illumination on his features. He did not look to Torn like a man who had just been rescued from certain death, but rather like one who has accepted the fact that he was not going to be "above snakes" much longer.

Torn slept fitfully, sitting propped up against another rock, his Winchester laid across his legs. Halfway through the night, Chapman went up the hill to relieve Codi, but the Apache scout never came down.

They were on the move again at first light, holding to the north side of the river, expecting to cut Santiago's trail in short order.

An hour after sunrise they saw the dust—many riders a few miles behind them. Codi took his horse from Alvarez and rode back to confirm what they all knew in their hearts.

When the scout returned, he needed only one word to explain.

"Vaqueros."

"How many?" asked Torn.

Codi opened and closed both hands, twice.

"Twenty against four," muttered Chapman. "Long odds."

"I've seen worse," said Torn.

CHAPTER 16

THIS TIME OF YEAR THE RIO GRANDE WAS LOW AND COULD BE crossed almost anywhere.

Sitting his horse on the brow of a ten-foot cutbank, Torn borrowed Chapman's field glasses and scanned the opposite side of the river. Just downriver, at the base of a fifty-foot sandstone bluff, was a stand of black cypress. Farther east, the river curled slowly southward. Beneath the trees, deadfall was strewn across the rocky riverbed. A draw provided access to the crest of the bluff.

In these situations, Torn's wartime experience as a cavalry commander served him well. A glance was all he needed to determine that in the trees was the place to make a stand. Plenty of cover. A good field of fire. He quickly formulated a plan.

"It's time we crossed into Mexico, gentlemen," he said, handing the field glasses back to Chapman. "We'll take cover in the trees yonder, catch them in the open as they cross after us." He turned in his saddle and fixed a steely gaze on Alvarez. "You said you have friends in that outfit. Are you willing to fight?"

Alvarez nodded. "They are willing to kill me."

Torn looked next at Chapman. "Any objections?"

"I don't like the idea of shooting at these men. They're just cowboys. They're following Flynn's orders. I doubt if a single one of them has any idea what's really going on."

"They work for Flynn, and Flynn's in league with Garza Santiago."

"But those vaqueros don't know that."

"If you'd like to stay here and try to explain the situation to them, be my guest," snapped Torn, provoked. "If I'm able when the fight is over, I'll come back across and bury what's left of you."

Chapman scowled. Thin-lipped, he put spurs to his horse. The animal lunged down the cutbank, stumbled, righted itself, and headed for the river at a gallop.

Shaking his head, Torn followed at a more sedate pace, letting his horse pick its way down the cutbank. Alvarez, back on Codi's mount, came along behind. The Apache scout jumped off the cutbank and landed with the agility of a big cat, proceeding on to the river at a ground-eating lope.

The crossing presented no difficulty. At its deepest point, the river reached no higher than their stirrups. On the other side, Torn dismounted, drew the Winchester from the saddle boot, and handed the reins to Codi.

"Take the horses over the rim of the bluff," he told the scout. "Hold them there. The vaqueros will cross right here when they see our sign. Once they find out what we're up to, though, I reckon they'll try to flank us. When they move, you move. Keep them busy until we can climb out of here and reach the horses. And kill their horses, if you can."

"Kill their horses!" exclaimed Chapman, aghast.

"They'll have a rough time of it, following us on foot," said Torn.

Codi glanced at Chapman before moving in response to Torn's orders. The lieutenant nodded tacit permission, and only then did the Apache proceed to lead the horses through the trees, making for the draw that would provide him access to the top of the bluff.

"I have no weapon," said Alvarez, without enthusiasm.

Torn tossed him the Winchester. "We'll take up positions back away from the river, say twenty paces. These rocks will slow down the ones who manage to get across. Spread out, and don't fire until they're in the middle of the river." He looked sharply at Chapman. "That suit you, Lieutenant?"

"I'm not a lieutenant any longer," was Chapman's sour reply. "So I guess we'll do this your way. You've been doing a damn fine job so far, and you seem to like giving orders."

Without a word in response, Torn headed deeper into the stand of cypress, picking his way across the rocks and deadfall. He found a good spot among the knees of a massive tree. Alvarez settled in thirty feet to his left, and Chapman picked a place a little farther off to his right.

There weren't many trees between Torn and the river, so he had the prospect of fairly unobstructed shooting. Drawing the Colt Peacemaker, he half cocked it, rolled the cylinder on his arm, and blew a film of dust off the firing pin before letting the hammer down.

Leaning a shoulder against the trunk of the tree, he

stretched his legs out between the cypress knees and tried to relax while he waited. He watched the morning sunlight dance on the surface of the Rio Grande, scintillating like a million diamonds.

He looked behind him once, to spot Codi leading the horses along a narrow game trail winding up through the steep draw gouged into the face of the bluff. The scout had tied the three mounts together in a way that permitted them to climb single file—the reins of the second and third horse secured to the saddle horn of the animal preceding it.

Torn knew instinctively that he could rely on the Apache. Codi was the kind you wanted on your side in a scrape. Too bad, thought Torn, that he couldn't have trusted Alvarez to hold the horses; to have Codi down here in the thick of the imminent fight would have been a real comfort. But Torn wasn't sure about the vaquero. He had a suspicion Alvarez would have dusted out with all the horses as soon as the shooting started.

He heard the muted thunder of distant horses at the gallop. A shudder racked him with sudden, unexpected violence. The sound sent a chill down his spine. After a moment's bewilderment, he realized why.

It was the sound of his dream.

Nightmare, really. The sound of the horses ridden by the four faceless men bearing down on Melony Hancock as she reached out to him, called out his name, and as he turned his back on her to embrace Meg Slaughter.

Torn cursed, a soft but fervent epithet.

They appeared at the top of the cutbank across the river, a hundred yards away. Twenty of them, as Codi had said. Dust swirled around them. Sunlight glinted off buckles and conchos and the metal of rifles and pistols. They paused on the cutbank's rim, checking the sign, the river, the stand of cypress. Torn didn't see Flynn among them. That was no surprise. Flynn wasn't one to fight his own fights. Not when he could pay other men to die for him.

Seeing the tracks they were following angle down to the river, the men of the Coronado Cattle Company spurred their foam-flecked horses down off the cutbank and headlong into the Rio Grande.

They spread out, forming a wedge, as they progressed deeper into the river. Plumes of spray shot skyward, horses snorted and blew, some of the men shouted, exhorting their ponies on.

Fifty yards.

Chapman was right, mused Torn. To a degree, at least. These vaqueros weren't bad men. They were ordinary cowboys, doing a job their boss had told them to do. Good soldiers, who didn't ask for reasons why. Just like the men in blue Torn had fought for four long and bloody years. He had harbored no animosity toward the federal troops who had confronted him on a dozen battlefields, and he found he harbored none toward these Coronado men, either.

But he had no doubt Flynn's boys had come to shoot, not talk. This was war, and a man did what he had to in order to live. That meant killing the men who were trying to kill you, and good or bad didn't enter into the equation.

Twenty yards.

Almost across the river.

Cold, calm, deliberate, Torn drew a bead on one of the vaqueros riding at the point of the wedge and squeezed the trigger.

CHAPTER 17

THE VAQUERO SLUMPED FORWARD, THEN SLIPPED SIDEWAYS out of the saddle to sprawl in the Rio Grande shallows.

To Torn's left, Alvarez began firing the Winchester. To his right, Chapman's army-issue Spencer carbine spoke. The Coronado men were caught completely by surprise. Several more plunged into the river, and only one of them came up shooting.

Amateurs, thought Torn. He himself would have sent a scout ahead to check the cypress grove before crossing the river. But none of Flynn's riders had his kind of experience, and now they were paying the price.

Yet they wouldn't quit. They didn't go running back across the river. These were men, most of them, who had been born and raised in the *brasada,* country that did not breed or brook weaklings and cowards.

Caught off guard, the Coronado men were quick to

recover and began firing back. Their bullets whined off rocks and slapped into the cypress knees.

Torn respected their grit, if not their wisdom. It was almost impossible to shoot accurately on horseback, and most of the vaqueros were staying in their saddles. That was habit. They lived forked on a horse; they worked and sometimes ate and slept there. It was only natural that they were inclined to fight from the saddle. But their mounts were not trained to stand steady with guns going off all around, as good cavalry ponies were, and Flynn's riders had to split their concentration between shooting and staying on horses that were reverting to their mustang ways in all the noise and confusion.

Sooner or later, Torn knew, one of them would wise up and either pull back or dismount and seek cover among the trees and rocks and deadfall. Then the others would follow suit. Until then, he took advantage of the situation and fired into the melee, picking his targets. Two more vaqueros toppled into the roiling red waters of the Rio Grande. Alvarez and Chapman accounted for a couple more. Torn began feeling optimistic about the outcome of this set-to. They were fast whittling down the odds.

Then Alvarez lost his nerve, broke, and ran.

In that moment the tide of battle turned. Flynn's riders once more became the hunters. Several spurred their horses forward in pursuit of Alvarez, out of the shallows and onto the rocks. But their mounts slipped and stumbled on the water-smoothed stones beneath the cypress trees, making poor time.

Seeing their *compadres* advance, the rest of the Coronado men surged forward. One by one they saw the light and dismounted. Directly in front of Torn, a vaquero jumped out of the saddle and turned his horse to use the animal as a shield, resting his rifle in the dip of the saddle, aiming at Torn's position. Torn didn't give him time to get off a shot. He fired once and the horse went down, dead before it hit the ground. Stunned, the Coronado man just stood there, frozen for a fatal instant. Torn fired again. The bullet struck the vaquero squarely in the chest, hurling him backward.

Reloading, Torn glanced to his left just as Alvarez spun and fell, a bullet in the back. Though he did not know Alvarez, and his instincts had warned him— rightly, as it turned out—not to trust the man, Torn was angered. He despised backshooters. The vaquero responsible for bringing Alvarez down let go a shout of exultation, which provoked Torn even further. He shifted his position slightly, drew a bead. The Colt Peacemaker jumped in his hand. The man who had accounted for Alvarez was in turn accounted for.

With Alvarez down, the Coronado men turned their attention on Torn and Chapman. A few were still mounted, but most were on foot now, scattered under the trees, some deeper into the grove than others. They were firing at Torn's position from several directions at once, and for a moment all Torn could do was lie flat on his belly between bullet-splintered cypress knees and keep his head down. Those on foot were using cover to close in, darting from deadfall to tree, shooting as they moved.

The situation was grim, but Torn didn't panic. It occurred to him that maybe he had underestimated these men. They hadn't fled the ambush or tried a flanking maneuver; instead they'd put their heads down and bulled straight ahead.

Torn knew better than to try to run. That was certain death. His fate would be the same as Alvarez's. The vaquero's loss of nerve had cost him his life. And, many years before, Torn had made himself a solemn promise: he would not go down with a bullet in the back. It would not be said of him that he ran from a fight.

Then, as the Coronado men closed in on Torn, Codi dealt himself into the fray.

From the rim of the bluff, the Apache scout's Spencer barked twice. One of Flynn's riders somersaulted backward off his horse. A second, in the process of running from tree to tree, was knocked sideways in midstride by the impact of the 56/50 slug, landing on the rocks limp as a rag doll, dead eyes staring skyward, forever surprised.

The vaqueros were quick to comprehend where this new threat was coming from and some of them fired at the rimrock. But Codi gave them nothing to shoot at. All anyone down below could see was a wisp of gun smoke up yonder.

Again the tide of battle turned. Codi held the high ground and the Coronado men understood that they were sitting ducks. Those still mounted reined their horses sharply and made for the other side of the river like the devil himself was hot on their heels. The ones on foot either caught up a horse or legged it into the Rio Grande.

Seizing the initiative, Torn powered to his feet and ran to the nearest fallen vaquero—the one whose horse he had killed. He snatched up the dead man's repeating rifle, brought stock to shoulder, and fired.

A horse stumbled and fell in the shallows with a shrill scream. Torn worked the rifle's action, fired again. A second horse went down; another vaquero was hurled headlong into the river.

Hearing Chapman shouting hoarsely, Torn glanced to his right. The lieutenant was standing out in the open, yelling at him. Torn could not make out his words; guns were going off, men were shouting, and his ears were ringing. But he got the sense that Chapman was beside himself with rage.

"Shoot the horses, dammit!" yelled Torn, and went back to work.

From the rimrock, Codi was doing his part. Of the nine Coronado men who reached the American side of the Rio Grande, only two were mounted.

Torn emptied the repeater, threw it down, and fired his Colt until the hammer fell on an empty chamber. He did not expect to hit anything at that range with a sidegun. He wasn't really trying to hit anything any longer. Flynn's men had their backs to him now and he wasn't a backshooter. He simply wanted to prevent them from entertaining second thoughts about retreat.

His strategy worked. Minutes later the only thing left of the surviving vaqueros was dun-colored dust hanging in the hot, still air.

Drawing deep breaths, Torn reloaded the Colt and took a long look around. A half-dozen riderless horses wandered through the trees. Dead men and mounts were scattered in the shallows and on the blood-splattered stones beneath the cypress trees. A wounded man groaned. Torn moved, letting the sound guide him.

The man was curled up in a ball, arms wrapped tightly around his midsection. The stones around him looked as though they had been dipped in crimson paint. He was ghastly pale, and more blood trickled out of the corner of his mouth. He looked up at Torn with pain-narrowed eyes, and at the Colt in Torn's hand.

"No muerte," he gasped.

Torn felt no animosity toward the vaquero. Only pity. The anger in his heart was focused on Aloysius Flynn, for sending good men to their deaths. He holstered the

Peacemaker. The vaquero was gut-shot. Dying by slow, agonizing degrees, and there wasn't a thing that could be done for him.

"Torn!"

He turned to see Chapman coming toward him.

"You cold-blooded bastard!" raged Chapman. "Killing horses, for God's sake!"

"We won't have to worry about them coming after us now," said Torn. "Why don't you make yourself useful and catch up those horses yonder? We'll take them along with us." He started to turn away, had a thought, and turned back. "And while you're at it, find a dead man who's about your build. You need to get rid of that uniform. We're in Mexico now, and you need to dress for the occasion."

CHAPTER 18

TORN CHECKED ON ALVAREZ AND CONFIRMED THAT THE MAN was dead. Retrieving his Winchester, he moved on to each fallen Coronado vaquero in turn. Six were dead. One had only minutes left among the ranks of the living. Two were unaccounted for, and Torn assumed they had been swept downriver. Alive or dead, he didn't know, and he didn't concern himself about it.

There was one wounded vaquero that Torn thought would probably recover. The man had been shot in the leg. He was sitting up against the trunk of a cypress, smoking a roll-your-own. His pistol lay in his lap. He didn't reach for the gun as Torn neared, and Torn did not draw the Colt from its holster, though he did rest his hand on the bone-inlaid butt, ready to draw and fire at the vaquero's first hostile move.

"No te preocupas," said the Coronado man. Realizing

Torn might not understand, he added. "My *pistola,* she is empty, hombre."

"Throw it away," said Torn, gesturing with his left hand.

Smiling, the vaquero complied. *"Como se llama, señor?"*

"What?"

"I was just asking your name."

"Why?"

"I would just like to know the name of the man who kills me."

"Then you don't need to know more."

The Coronado man tilted his head and glanced sidelong at Torn, as though he suspected Torn was playing a joke on him. "You mean you are going to let me live?"

"Long as you don't try something."

"What can I do? The bullet, it broke the bone in my leg. I am not going anywhere for a while, I think. I can do nothing."

"Guess I'll leave you a horse."

"You killed many of my *compadres,* hombre. So why is it you don't kill me, too?"

"What did Flynn tell you to do about us?"

"He said Alvarez had betrayed our *segundo,* Frank Robles, and the other three the bandits hanged. He told us to bring him the bodies of Alvarez and the men who had helped him escape. We did not ask why. You do not ask Señor Flynn why he wants you to do something. You just do it."

"That was all he said?"

"He told us not to come back without the bodies."

Which was the reason, mused Torn, that the Coronado men had fought with such determination. "Alvarez wasn't working with Santiago. Your boss is."

"Señor Flynn?"

"You don't believe me."

The man shrugged. "It doesn't matter. I cannot go back anyway."

Torn nodded. "Just ride on. Best way to stay alive."

"*Sí*. You give good advice, I think."

Torn left him, met up with Codi at the mouth of the draw. The Apache scout was leading the cavalry horses. His Spencer carbine was shoulder-racked.

"Good shooting," congratulated Torn. "You saved my bacon."

As always, the Apache was impassive. He pointed with his chin across the river, in the direction taken by the surviving Coronado men. "They will not come back."

"I'd be surprised."

They walked on to the spot where Chapman was holding the Coronado mounts. The lieutenant had exchanged his uniform for vaquero garb: sombrero, a dark green *chaqueta,* concho-studded chaps. Torn spotted the bullet hole in the jacket and figured it was recent. Codi just stared. The scout could not remember ever having seen Chapman out of uniform. The clothes fit, but Chapman nonetheless looked very uncomfortable.

"We'll be taking all the horses but one," said Torn.

"Why leave one?"

Torn sighed. Chapman was bound and determined to question every decision he made.

"Because I said so."

"We should bury the dead."

"No."

"There's not a shred of common decency left in you, is there, Judge?"

"I doubt it."

"It's only right to bury them," insisted Chapman, obstinate.

"They're dead. They don't care anymore. Besides, the longer we dally here, the further away Santiago takes Meg."

"I wish you'd thought about that when we went off to pay Flynn a visit. If we hadn't done that, we wouldn't be standing here discussing dead men."

"You want to win a war, you better know who your enemies are."

"Just why are you here, Judge? I'd like to know. You got some ideas about Meg Slaughter?"

"If I do, it's none of your business."

"The hell it isn't!"

They glowered at one another, fists clenched, and there would have been another fight on the Rio Grande that day if Codi had not intervened.

The Apache scout turned and swung into the saddle of his horse without touching foot to stirrup. Tapping the heels of his desert moccasins against the animal's flanks, he maneuvered the horse forward, between Torn and Chapman. He offered each man the reins to his horse.

"We go," he said.

Torn looked up into Codi's guarded black eyes and came to his senses. With a curt nod, he accepted the reins and mounted up. Smoldering, Chapman did likewise. A hostile silence prevailed as they departed the cypress grove, heading east by south, each man leading a pair of horses branded with the mark of the Coronado Cattle Company.

Two hours later they found sign—unmistakably Garza Santiago's bandit army, southbound. Torn ventured a guess that the tracks were a day old, and Codi confirmed this with a nod.

"Let's ride," urged Chapman. "We've each got two extra horses. We can ride a horse until he's bottomed out and then switch our tack to another. We can go day and night that way without stopping. We'll sleep in the saddle."

"Ride horses into the ground?" Torn was sarcastic. "I can't believe I'm hearing this from you, Chapman."

Chapman stood in his stirrups, staring south at a horizon marred by the shimmer of heat haze, as though he hoped to see far beyond the range of human vision and spot Meg Slaughter, alive and well.

"There's a town about a day's ride due south," he said. "Tres Cruces. Might be that Santiago will linger there. He's not worried about anybody being after him. He doesn't have to hole up out in the malpais; he knows he's beyond the reach of the U.S. Cavalry."

The lieutenant settled in his saddle and dug spur, an expression of grim resolve on his dust-caked features. Codi followed, and Torn brought up the rear, hoping that Chapman was right about Santiago lingering in Tres Cruces and wondering what three men could do against a hundred if it turned out that he was right.

CHAPTER 19

"THE SINS OF THE FATHER," MOANED THE OLD WOMAN. She was rocking slightly in the rickety chair, her gnarled hands clasped tightly in her lap, shaking her head. "This village was cursed that day, twenty years ago, when—"

Her bare feet making no sound on the hard-packed earthen floor of the drab, one-room *choza,* the young woman crossed to lay a comforting hand on the *anciana's* bony shoulder. "Hush, *tía.* Do not speak of it. That was a long time ago."

"Not for the spirits who still haunt this place," insisted the old one. The flickering yellow light cast by the candle on the table accentuated all the creases in her cheeks and forehead, deep lines etched by ninety years of hardship. "I warned them not to do that terrible thing. They would not listen. Not even your father, Clara." She touched the young woman's arm with tender affection. Her eyes, sunk deep in their sockets, glimmered with tears. "Now you must pay for his sin."

"I will not be harmed, Tía Sophia," assured Clara, rendering up a brave smile. "Santiago himself wishes to see me. Tomorrow they will go. It is always the same. They come and they go. They are no worse than the *rurales.*"

The door flew open on its leather hinges, and the bandit who had been waiting impatiently outside stepped in, his big Chihuahua spurs jangling. He was slapping his leg with a braided quirt.

"Hurry, woman," he growled. "Garza does not like to be kept waiting."

Clara lovingly kissed her aunt on the cheek. She wanted to say something else reassuring, but she didn't trust her voice. Summoning every ounce of courage she could find within her, she walked out of the hut, her chin at a defiant angle, ignoring the bandit who glowered at her as she passed.

The *choza* was one of those that fronted on the square of Tres Cruces. Night had fallen hours ago. A night of horror for the people of the village. The square was filled with the shadowy shapes of men and horses.

Santiago had loosed his dogs of war.

Branching off the square was a brief and miserable excuse for a *calle,* and down this Clara walked, her escort behind her. The street ended abruptly at the edge of a field of withered corn. The crops, in the best of times, were kept barely alive by brackish water supplied to an irrigation ditch by a notoriously unreliable *riachuelo.* This time of year, the stream was as dry as the bones of a man long dead. It had been so for many, many days. The crops were dying.

Near the end of the street, adjacent to the parched fields, were a few dwellings somewhat larger and better than the average. They had two or three rooms and real floors. One, the home of the alcalde, was even encompassed by a low wall—crumbling in disrepair, but a wall, nonetheless.

No one in Tres Cruces could be considered well-off. Not even the alcalde. Everyone was poor. It was merely a matter of degree. And tonight they were being rendered poorer by the minute. Between the bandits who called themselves revolutionaries and the ones who called themselves government soldiers, Clara thought it was a wonder the common people could survive at all. Both sides claimed they fought for the campesino, when in fact all they did was take what little the poor people had.

For all her courage, Clara trembled as she walked the street. She glanced back once. Her rifle-toting escort leered at her. She knew he was walking behind her because he liked to watch the sway of her trim hips beneath the peasant skirt she wore. Lust gave his unshaven, brutish features an ugly cast. Clara surmised that he resented having this duty to perform while his friends were allowed to ride roughshod through the village. He wanted to have fun, too, and undoubtedly he wanted to start with her. But he refrained from forcing himself on her. It wasn't common decency that deterred him. It was fear. Fear of the consequences should he be caught satisfying his desires rather than obeying Santiago's orders.

Some of Santiago's men huddled in groups along the street, drunk and lewd and boisterous. Others were forcing their way into the meager homes of the villagers, taking the pulque and mescal, the food, what few personal belongings were worth anything.

And they took other things. Before Clara's very eyes, three bandits dragged thirteen-year-old Maria Sanchez from the arms of her hysterical mother. A fourth bandit pistol-whipped Maria's father, when he moved to rescue his daughter. Maria was carried, screaming, into the terror-filled shadows between two *casitas*. Sobbing, the mother sank to her knees beside the bloodied body of her husband, slumped in the doorway of their wretched dwelling. The bandits laughed harshly at Maria's futile resistance. Their laughter, and the sobs of the mother, tore at Clara's heart. Fighting back tears of rage and frustration, Clara hurried past.

Clara was a realist. She knew she was pretty—they said she was the prettiest girl in the village. So she tried to convince herself that she was lucky to be the one selected by Santiago. Otherwise she would have shared poor Maria's fate.

Half a dozen men stinking of pulque and sweat lounged along the wall fronting the alcalde's house. This house, the best in Tres Cruces, had naturally been commandeered by Santiago. The alcalde and his family had been tossed out into the street.

Clara made for the gate in the wall, but the bandits blocked her way. She knew twisting despair. Her escort protested, but his *compadres* just laughed and pushed him away. He made belligerent talk, but took no action. Clara closed her ears to graphically lewd suggestions. As she tried to get past them one man grabbed her roughly around the waist. Her control snapped. She clawed and kicked, screaming hoarsely. The bandits merely laughed. She gasped as rough, groping hands crushed her breasts, and winced at rancid breath as one man tried to kiss her.

A brusque order curtailed the lust-thick laughter of her assailants, and Clara found herself thrown violently to the ground as Santiago's most trusted lieutenant,

Ochoa, made a timely appearance. Ochoa cursed the sullen bandits.

"Idiots!" he railed, contemptuous. "Animals! Bastards! I should kill you all right here. It would save Garza the trouble. He has sent for this woman. Do you understand? Do you think he wants the marks of your filthy hands on her, or the foul stench of you when she comes to him?"

The bandits backed off, sobered by a threat they knew was all too real. Ochoa helped Clara to her feet. She fought to regain her composure as he took her into the casa, and into the presence of Garza Santiago.

Santiago waited in the front room. His booted feet were propped up on the mahogany table that had been the alcalde's pride and joy—far and away the best piece of furniture in Tres Cruces. It's arrival by wagon from Veracruz had caused much excitement, Clara recalled.

Now Santiago's spurs gouged huge ugly scars in the table's polished surface. His arms were crossed, his chin lowered, and his eyes were dark and muddy pools of seething emotion.

"Leave us," he growled at Ochoa.

Ochoa evacuated the room.

Clara stood rigidly, fighting an irrational urge to run. There was no place to run.

"Pour me a drink, *mujer.*"

On the table, beside a coal-oil lamp that provided the room's only illumination, was a bottle of Baconara and a pewter cup. There also, beside Santiago's pistol, were bulging saddlebags.

Clara stood rooted to the floor.

"I am not in the habit of giving the same order twice, woman," warned Santiago.

She moved timidly to the table, picked up the fan-shaped bottle. Santiago watched her like a hawk. Clara poured, put the bottle down, handed the cup filled with brandy to Santiago. A dry smile touched his lips.

"You didn't spill a drop. *Bueno*. This is too good to waste."

"Why do you do this to my village?" asked Clara.

Santiago shrugged. "In war, the innocent suffer. It has always been so. We fight for you, die for you. The least you can do is provide for our needs." He swung his legs down, leaned forward in the chair to stare moodily at the brandy in the pewter cup. "Do you think I enjoy watching your people suffer? My men are not much better than animals, I admit. But they are good fighters. I must give them what they want or they will not follow me. Once we throw Díaz out, things will get better. We will not need such men anymore."

He looked up at her, surprised at his own candor, and tried to gauge her reaction. For a moment Clara saw through this emotional breach and caught a glimpse of the inner man. Then the breach closed, and Santiago's eyes became dull and dead and sleepy.

"You really believe in the revolution," said Clara.

"Of course. Díaz is a butcher."

"And you would be *el presidente*."

"Who knows."

"But nothing would change," Clara declared. "Then there would be other men who would want to throw you out and become *el presidente*. And they would ride with the same kind of men you ride with. And they would come here and do the same thing you are doing to my village. Some things never change."

Santiago slammed his fist down on the table and jumped to his feet, overturning his chair. Clara jumped.

"I believe in the revolution!" he snarled, enraged. Then, as suddenly as it had come, his anger ebbed, and he smiled. "I like you. You are not afraid to speak your mind. Here." He unstrapped one of the saddlebags and took from it a gold coin. Leaning across the table, he placed it in front of her. "Twenty dollars American. Take it. It will buy many things."

Clara refused to look at the double eagle on the table in front of her. All she could think about was Maria Sanchez.

"You cannot buy what your men have taken from the people of this village. Just go away. Leave us alone. We have done nothing to you."

Santiago sauntered around the table. "I cannot leave. Not yet. I am to meet a man here. He is going to sell me the guns I need to win."

"You have guns." As Santiago drew near, Clara forced herself to stand her ground. She wanted to run. But she refused to show fear, and she even managed, somehow, not to cringe as he reached out to cup her chin in his hand.

"Yes, I have guns. And I have had many women. But you . . . you are no ordinary woman. I knew that the moment I saw you. And these guns I am to buy. They are not ordinary guns."

His hand caressed her neck, her shoulder, traveled down her arm as he spoke. Clara shuddered involuntarily. Laughing, Santiago grabbed her around the waist and pulled her roughly to him. She turned her face away when he tried to kiss her. Amused, he grabbed her hair, wrenched her head back, and bruised her lips with his.

Clara had resigned herself to her fate—or so she had thought until this moment. She had promised herself that she would at least get through the ordeal with dignity. She had told herself she would not fight or beg or cry because none of that would do any good. Santiago wanted her, and he would take her. It was as certain as death.

But when Santiago tried to force his tongue into her mouth, something snapped inside her. A sound like the keening wail of a cornered cat escaped her, and she slapped him so hard he rocked back on his heels.

Cold fury surged through Santiago. Snarling, he hit her in the face with his fist. She fell, blacked out, and came to with Santiago straddling her and tearing like a mad beast at her dress. Her mouth was full of blood, and she spat into his face. Santiago clutched her throat with one hand and began to squeeze. She flailed wildly beneath him, but his weight held her down. Her lungs aching for air, Clara clawed at his face. Santiago squeezed harder. She saw her own death in his blazing eyes.

She didn't hear the knock on the door above the thunder in her ears, but Santiago did. He ignored it. A more insistent rapping followed.

"Jefe!"

It was Ochoa.

"Go away!" growled Santiago, still trying to choke the life out of Clara. "I'm busy!"

"But, *jefe!* The Englishman . . ."

Santiago swore. Disgusted, he let go of Clara and stood just as the door opened.

A whiff of lavender preceded the entrance of a thin, pale man clad in a blue clawhammer coat, ruffled white shirt, duck trousers, and half boots. He entered with a haughty air, swinging a gold-ferruled walking stick. When he saw Clara half naked on the floor, and Santiago leaning against the table with blood on his face where Clara had scratched him, he pulled up short. Using the tip of the walking stick, he tilted his bowler hat to a jaunty angle and smirked.

"I say, old chap, did I interrupt something?"

CHAPTER 20

THEY COULD SEE THE LIGHTS OF TRES CRUCES TWO MILES away, across the inky-black expanse of a sagebrush valley, against the backdrop of rugged peaks that looked like jagged teeth tearing into the star-spangled fabric of the night sky.

"I wonder if Santiago is there," murmured Chapman, after they had sat their horses a few minutes in silence, speaking what was on all their minds.

"One of us has to find out," said Torn. "Wait for me here. I'll be back before daybreak."

"Codi would stand a better chance," said Chapman.

He wasn't concerned with Torn's welfare—he just didn't think Torn could do the job. And if Torn got caught, and Santiago was alerted—assuming the bandit leader *was* holed up down there in Tres Cruces—then it would make Meg's rescue that much more difficult to accomplish.

To Chapman's astonishment, Codi said no.

The lieutenant couldn't believe his ears. He didn't know what to say. He just stared at Codi, thunderstruck. Sitting his horse, the Apache scout watched the lights of Tres Cruces floating in a sea of blackness. He had done away with his blue army tunic, with the corporal's stripes he had been so proud of.

"I cannot," he said flatly, knowing his friend expected —and deserved—more by way of explanation. He had never before refused to do what Chapman had asked of him, and he was in a turmoil now after having done so.

But he could not bring himself to open up to Chapman.

The pain cut too deeply.

Instead he dismounted and led his horses away, along the rim of the rise where they had paused for their first look at Tres Cruces.

"He isn't afraid," said Chapman. He was stunned, but not too stunned that he could not rise to Codi's defense.

"I know that," replied Torn. "He must have a good reason. Let it go at that. I'll be back."

"No. I'm better qualified. I'll go."

"Better qualified? How do you figure?"

"For one thing, I've been to Tres Cruces. When I rode with my father, mustanging, we used to come through here every now and then. For another, I speak Spanish and you don't. And finally I'm dressed for the occasion. Remember? Those good enough reasons, *Mister* Torn?"

Torn had to admit to himself that they were all very compelling reasons indeed. He wasn't, however, about to admit this to Chapman. The lieutenant could indeed pass for a Mexican, if the inspection wasn't too close.

"Okay," said Torn. "Just remember one thing. All we want to do now is determine whether Santiago is down there. Don't try getting Meg out alone, if he is. No heroics."

"You're worried I might get killed?"

"Not particularly. But I do worry that you might get Meg killed."

Fuming, Chapman bit his tongue. He handed Torn the reins of his two spare mounts and without another word urged the Coronado horse he was riding down into the valley.

Torn dismounted, loosened the cinches of the horses in his keeping, and gave them each some water, pouring from his canteen into the crown of his hat. They had come across a *tinaja*—a rock tank fed by a year-round seeping spring—twenty miles back, so water was not a problem. They could get more of it all along the way if they had to follow Santiago deeper into Mexico; Garza had a lot of men and horses in his entourage, and Torn figured he knew where all the water holes in this godforsaken desert were to be found.

Nonetheless Torn was concerned about the horses. They were hardy stock, desert mustangs, but they needed grain and rest. Torn knew that if by some miracle they managed to rescue Meg Slaughter, there was a very good chance they'd have to hightail it north for the border with a pack of bloodthirsty *bandoleros* breathing down their necks. If their horses failed them, they would be doomed.

Shortly after Chapman's departure, Codi returned along the rim. He looked for a long time down into the valley where Chapman had gone, and though he wore no expression, Torn sensed his guilt.

"He'll make it," said Torn.

If Codi heard, he gave no sign.

Torn used a reata taken from the saddle of one of the Coronado horses to make a picket line, tying both ends to heavy rocks, and then securing the reins of his three mounts and Chapman's pair of extras to the lariat. Drawing the Winchester from its saddle boot, he stretched out on a U.S. Army blanket.

Codi secured his horses to the line, then sat on his heels a few feet away from Torn.

Eyes closed, hands behind his head, Torn said, "If you want to tell me, go ahead."

"When I was *ish-ke-ne*—a little boy—my family was killed. For many years my people at war with the *Nakai-Ye*—the Mexicans. One day they come, the *Nakai-Ye* who live down there in Tres Cruces. They say they want peace. They say come to our village. We will treat you as honored guests. We will eat and drink together, they tell us. We will give you gifts. We will be friends forever more. All they asked was that we would not raid their village again.

"My *dagotai* did not trust their words. But our *jefe* would not listen to my father's warning, and he took our people into Tres Cruces. The people of the village gave us much food, much mescal. There was dancing and singing. And when all our warriors were drunk, the men of the village fell upon them, and the women and children as well. They used guns, knives, clubs, anything that could kill. I saw my father die. My mother and brother, too. A few of us got away. But most of my people were butchered that night. Then the villagers sold their scalps to the *Nakai-Ye* soldiers. They paid good money for Indian scalps."

By now Torn was up on one elbow, eyes wide open.

"I understand," he said. "I, too, lost my family. I saw my brother killed."

"The *Nakai-Ye* are my enemy. Always."

"You can kill every Mexican you run across and it won't change anything. I've let what happened in my past rule the way I lived my life for a dozen years. I'm just now beginning to see that you have to live for the future."

"I have no future," was Codi's flat reply. "The Apache people have no future. Sometimes in the night I hear the cries of owls. They are the voices of my father and mother and brother. They call out to me." He pointed with his chin at the distant lights of Tres Cruces. "When I go there, I go to avenge their deaths. It must be so. This is why I do not go tonight. The lieutenant, he is my *schicho*—my good friend. He comes to save the woman. I have promised to help him do this. When it is done, then I will come back and do what I have to do."

Torn lay back down and closed his eyes again. He tried to sleep, but Codi's grim story kept him awake for quite some time. And when he finally did sleep, he dreamed.

At first it was the same dream as before, down to the very last soul-wounding detail.

Only this time he saw the faces of three of the four shadow riders bearing down on the helpless Melony Hancock.

Santiago.

Flynn.

And Meg Slaughter . . .

In his dream he whirled, and where Meg had stood the first time, Chapman stood now. The lieutenant's gun was drawn and aimed at him. Torn could tell by the look of sheer hate on Chapman's face that the man was going to pull the trigger.

But Torn didn't care. For some reason he felt compelled to turn back and look again at the four riders. Because somehow he knew he would recognize the fourth rider, too. A sense of dread overpowered him.

He didn't want to see the face of the fourth rider, yet he had to turn and look. . . .

He turned back.

And woke up with a sob caught in his throat, his body drenched with sweat.

Codi was sitting cross-legged ten feet away, watching him.

"You hear them," said the Apache.

"What?" asked Torn, disoriented.

"The owls."

"Yes." Torn sighed, taking a deep breath. "I think I did."

CHAPTER 21

"YOU BRING THE GATLING GUNS, DARBY?" ASKED SANTIAGO.

"Naturally, old boy. I'm as good as my word. You know that. My credentials are impeccable, my references unimpeachable. Why, I've been doing business for years with certain of your counterparts. Mendoza. Soldado. Ask them, if you wish. I have never betrayed a trust, or double-crossed a business associate."

Santiago sneered. "They would have cut your throat if you had tried. So will I, Englishman, if you try to cheat me."

The dandy looked affronted. "Dear fellow, I wouldn't dream of it."

"So show me the guns."

"I do hope you won't mind terribly, but I would very much like to see the money first."

Santiago experimented with a bellicose glower, wondering if he could intimidate this man. Darby certainly looked like the sort who could be easily intimidated. But the Englishman did not seem at all bothered. His smile was both superior and shallow—it failed to reach his eyes, which did not flinch away from Santiago's.

Dropping the belligerent act, Santiago chuckled. He reached across the table for the saddlebags, tossed them at the Englishman. They landed at Darby's feet with a heavy thud punctuated by the rich jingle of coins.

Darby raised an eyebrow, bent, and picked up the saddlebags. He brought them back to the table. Setting down his walking stick, he opened one of the panniers, removed a sack, opened it, and extracted one gold double eagle.

"Upon my word," he murmured. "How lovely."

"Forty thousand American dollars," said Santiago. "Two thousand double eagles. Count them if you want."

Darby saw the coin Santiago had tried to give Clara. He picked it up.

"Including this one, by any chance?"

"You have your money. Now I want what I paid for. Twenty Gatling guns, and all the ammunition you promised."

"Quite." The dandy dropped both coins in the sack, replaced the sack in the pannier. Then he crossed in front of Santiago to stand beside Clara, who was sitting up now, trying to hold her damaged *camisa* in place, arms crossed over her breasts.

"Allow me," said Darby, and offered a hand. She took it, and he helped her to her feet. He turned a wry smile on Santiago. "You have exquisite taste in women, I must say, Garza, but awfully poor manners. You haven't introduced me to the lady. Darby Yarrow, ma'am, at your service."

Clara stared. She had never seen a man who dressed,

talked, or acted like this one. Though she was grateful for his timely arrival, she didn't trust him. He was obviously Santiago's ally, so she could expect no real help from him. But beyond that, there was something sinister about him. Behind that fancy facade was a man every bit as cruel and unprincipled as Garza Santiago.

"The woman is none of your business," declared Santiago.

"Forgive me. Instinct, my dear chap. Damsel in distress and all that, you know."

"The guns, Englishman."

Darby Yarrow bestowed a rakehell smile on Clara before returning to the table to retrieve the saddlebags. These he slung over a shoulder.

"They are in a safe place, not far from here, and well guarded. I shall bring them to you in the morning."

He started for the door.

The sound of a gun being cocked stopped him cold in his tracks. He looked back to find that Santiago was aiming a pistol at him.

"I take it those arrangements are not to your liking," remarked Yarrow, unruffled.

"No guns, no gold, amigo."

"Ah, well." Yarrow came back to the table, laid the saddlebags down, and reached for the bottle of Baconara. He examined the label with a connoisseur's eye. "Perhaps we should discuss it over a drink, like gentlemen." He glanced across at Clara. "But surely she doesn't need to be present."

"Don't worry about her," said Santiago. "She is one of my people. She knows if she talks I will cut out her tongue."

"He's going to kill me," Clara told Yarrow, as matter-of-fact as someone remarking on the weather.

"You don't mean it. Garza! What a waste."

"It is none of your business," said Santiago.

"So you've said. Still, I haven't survived this long by making the details of my delivery of certain merchandise public knowledge. In other words, my friend, if we are to talk about precisely where and when we will exchange your gold for my guns, I'm afraid it will have to be without this strumpet in the room."

Santiago let the hammer down on the pistol, snugged the weapon under his belt. "Ochoa!"

Santiago's right-hand man was waiting just outside the door. *"Jefe?"*

"Put this woman with the other one."

"Sí, jefe."

Clara was taken down a hallway to a door guarded by a *bandolero*. The door was locked from the outside. Ochoa turned the key, pushed the door open, and shoved Clara into the room.

"Garza will tend to you later, woman," said Ochoa, and laughed.

He slammed the door shut and locked it.

Clara turned to find herself in a spacious bedroom dominated by a large canopied bed. The room's only window had wrought-iron bars set into the adobe—the alcalde had taken steps to secure his belongings from his poorer neighbors—a security precaution to keep thieves out which tonight served perfectly to keep captives in.

The "other woman" Santiago had mentioned stood in a far corner, in the shadows at the edge of the light emitted by a lamp on the bedside table.

"Como se llama?" asked Clara.

Meg Slaughter was wearing a *camisa* and skirt much like Clara's; Santiago had provided them for her shortly after their arrival in the village, to replace her nightdress. Despite the clothing, Clara could tell she was an Anglo, and was surprised when Meg answered her question in very good Spanish.

"And your name?" asked Meg.

"Clara. This is my village. What are you doing here?"

"Santiago brought me."

"You are his woman?"

"His captive."

Clara moved closer. She could see that Meg was frightened, but holding up well.

"Where are you from?"

"Eagle Pass." Meg told her about the raid. When she spoke of her father, it was all she could do to keep from bursting into tears.

"Why did Santiago take you?"

"I don't know. I wish I knew. My father is a fairly rich man. . . ." Meg shrugged.

"But Santiago has much money already. He is buying guns with it even as we speak. Has Santiago . . . hurt you?"

"No. He hasn't laid a hand on me. And he has warned his men that if they try he will kill them."

"That is strange. You are *muy bonita.*"

"Can you help me, Clara? I must get away."

"I am a prisoner like you."

Overcome with despair, Meg slumped on the edge of the bed. Clara's heart went out to her. She sat beside Meg and put an arm around her shoulders. Then and there she resolved to help the woman escape.

"I will help you," she promised.

"How?"

"I don't know yet. But we will think of something."

"It's too dangerous. I shouldn't have asked you."

Clara smiled. "Santiago is going to use me while he is here, and when he is ready to leave, he will kill me."

"Kill you?" gasped Meg. "Why?"

"Because I hurt him. So you see, I have nothing to lose."

22

CHAPMAN DID NOT HAVE TO GET VERY CLOSE TO TRES Cruces to learn what he had come to learn. Santiago's men were swarming all over the village, and they were on their worst behavior. The streets were filled with men and horses. The bandits were looting every house and harassing every villager.

Leaving his horse three hundred yards out from the edge of town, the lieutenant slipped closer on foot. Alert for sentries, he saw none. That wasn't too surprising. Santiago was no soldier. He called his outlaw gang an army, and he thought of himself as a general of the revolution, but in fact his "army" was just a rabble of outlaws cut from the same diseased cloth as he.

And they were demonstrating that fact tonight in a very telling manner. Chapman felt sorry for the Tres Cruces campesinos. They were catching hell.

Hunkered down in the sagebrush, Chapman pondered his next move. He could return to Torn and Codi and the three of them could hash out a plan to slip into the village and rescue Meg. But where was Meg being held? They needed to know. Chapman resolved to press his luck and try to find out. And if the opportunity presented itself, he might even be able to get her out now. The prospect, though not very realistic, appealed to him. That would sure put one up on Judge Torn.

Logic and emotion warred within him. He knew this was not a game—a competition between two men vying for the attention of the same girl. It was a life-and-death situation. But he couldn't help being jealous and he couldn't abide the thought of Torn and Meg being together.

Of course, he mused, Torn had more to offer Meg than he, a deserter who was fair game for every sheriff, bounty hunter, and soldier in U.S. Army blue. He could not ask her to share the life of a fugitive.

But at least he could try to save her from Garza Santiago.

To the east of the village, a cornfield provided what appeared to be the best approach. It ran adjacent to the houses on that side of town. Chapman retraced his steps, retrieved his horse, and led it in a wide circle to the back side of the cornfield. Here he ground-hitched the horse before proceeding into the field.

He moved with caution, for the stalks were dry and withered, and they rustled and clacked together to betray his passage. The sound was loud in his ears, but he told himself it was unlikely the bandits having such a high time in the village would hear him. They were making too much noise of their own.

Lack of water had stunted the crop. Standing tall, he loomed head and shoulders above the corn. So he walked bent over, with the sombrero pushed back off his head to hang by its chinstrap down his back.

As luck would have it, when he reached the other side of the cornfield, he found himself a stone's throw from the alcalde's house.

He could look down a short street filled with boisterous men and nervous horses. But it was the Abbot & Downing coach in front of the alcalde's house that captured his attention. Two men sat up in the box, armed and watchful. Two more sat their horses on either side. They were all Mexicans, but they weren't Santiago's men. In fact, they were having nothing to do with the bandits. There were six good horses in the coach's hitch, and drapes of lavender velveteen covered the windows.

It was a fine rig, and not inexpensive, and Chapman wondered what the hell it was doing here.

But most of all he wondered how to find out where Meg was being held.

He could think of only one way.

Walk, bold as brass, down that street and ask someone.

He would ask where Santiago could be found, on the supposition that Santiago would be keeping Meg under his own watchful eye. With luck, the man he asked would be too drunk to pay very close attention to him.

It was a dangerous gamble, perhaps even suicidal.

But Chapman made up his mind to risk it. What did he have to lose?

Just as he was about to step out into the open, Santiago and Darby Yarrow emerged from the alcalde's house.

* * *

Chapman had never seen Garza Santiago in the flesh. Yet somehow he knew who the man was. And he *did* know the dandy in the clawhammer coat.

Darby Yarrow was Mexico's premier gunrunner. He worked out of Veracruz, had been in business for years. He took no sides, served no master but money. The Díaz government suspected him of supplying arms to the rebels, but turned a blind eye because of his connections in Europe and the United States. He could, and did, provide the government with the finest weapons money could buy.

"Tomorrow, then, old boy." Yarrow threw over his shoulder at Santiago. "And do remember to bring that lovely gold, won't you?"

"You remember to bring the Gatling guns," said Garza curtly. "If you do, you'll get your gold. If you don't, you'll get lead."

The Englishman chuckled. "How droll, my dear Garza. How droll."

As Yarrow climbed into the coach Chapman heard the rattle of cornstalks to his right.

Someone else was lurking in the cornfield.

He moved toward the sound, gun in hand—and almost stepped on Johnny Rand.

Johnny was flat on his belly, drawing a bead on Santiago with an old breech-loading Sharps.

He mistook Chapman for a *bandolero* and put up a fight. He almost cracked the lieutenant's skull with the barrel of the long gun.

"Johnny, for God's sake!" hissed Chapman as he wrestled with the youngster, thrashing through the corn and making such a racket that the lieutenant expected Santiago's entire bandit army to be on them like ticks on a redbone hound. "It's me, Johnny! Lieutenant Chapman!"

Johnny stopped struggling. The bullet wound in his arm hurting like hell, Chapman shot an anxious glance toward the village.

But no one had heard.

Yarrow's driver had whipped up the team; the coach was on the move, heading up the street in the direction of the square, and Santiago's men were firing exuberantly into the sky to send the Englishman off in typical bandit fashion. In addition to the shooting, lusty voices, slurred by too much mescal, were raised in a hoarse medley of *"Viva Santiago!"* and *"Viva Mexico!"*

The shouting and the gunfire had drowned out the noise Chapman and Johnny had made.

Chapman was so relieved he laughed out loud.

Johnny Rand wasn't laughing. He looked for Santiago in front of the alcalde's house, but the bandit leader had gone back inside.

"Dammit to hell!" swore Johnny, bitter. "I could've had him. I could've killed the son of a bitch that killed my pa if it hadn't been for you."

"If you'd pulled that trigger, we'd both be dead."

"I don't care!"

"Keep your voice down."

"I come all this way to pay Santiago back for what he done. And I aim to do just that."

Johnny started to get up, and Chapman realized the boy was fixing to embark on a one-man assault on the house where Santiago was staying. The lieutenant wrapped both arms around Johnny's legs and tackled him. Rand was primed to start fighting all over again, but this time Chapman socked him in the jaw first thing. Not hard enough to knock the youngster out, but sufficient to knock the fight out of him.

The lieutenant wrenched the Sharps out of the stunned youngster's grasp. "I don't blame you for wanting to kill Santiago," he said in a fierce whisper. "But you'll just have to wait until I get Meg out. Savvy?"

Johnny nodded.

"Got a horse?" asked Chapman.

"He went down a half day back. I trailed Santiago all the way from Eagle Pass. Rode all through the night. Didn't stop . . ."

"Rode your horse into the ground."

Again Johnny nodded. "I run most of the way after that."

Chapman was impressed by the youngster's grit. Johnny's clothes were dirty, tattered rags. Even his boots had been ripped by thorns. His cheeks were hollow, his eyes sunk deep in their sockets. No sleep and no food since leaving Eagle Pass—of this Chapman was certain.

"Come on, Johnny."

The lieutenant led the way out of the cornfield, carrying the Sharps, and found his horse where he had left it. He mounted, helped Johnny up behind him, and rode away from Tres Cruces, heading north for the high ground across the valley, where Torn and Codi were waiting.

It was hard, turning his back on Meg, knowing she was somewhere close. But suddenly a full-blown plan had leaped into his agile mind. Seeing the gunrunner, Darby Yarrow, had planted the seed.

He thought he knew now how to get Meg away from Santiago.

CHAPTER 23

WHEN HE SAW JOHNNY RAND, THE FIRST THING TORN wanted to know was how Burton Slaughter was doing.

"He was okay when I left," replied Johnny, hungrily consuming the hardtack Chapman had provided. "But I took out the same day you all did."

"The boy's been through hell just for a shot at Santiago," remarked Chapman. "And he was a prayer away from pulling the trigger when I found him."

Torn was angry at Johnny, and proud of him at the same time. Angry, because he believed Santiago was the only thing standing between Meg and certain death at the hands of the *bandoleros*. Johnny had been a heartbeat away from killing Santiago, which would have left Meg unprotected. He was proud of the youngster's feat: riding day and night a hundred miles without respite, and pressing on even after his horse had gone down, leaving him afoot in the middle of the malpais.

Revenge had seen him through. Torn knew all too well how revenge could do that. It had been the key to his own survival during the sixteen months of starvation and brutality he had endured at Point Lookout as a Confederate prisoner of war. When all the other reasons for living had seemed inadequate, the desire to repay Karl Schmidt for the torment the sadistic Yankee sergeant had bestowed upon him had kept Torn going.

Yes, he knew how powerful a motivating force vengeance could be.

"Santiago's buying guns," said Chapman. "He met a man named Darby Yarrow tonight." He told Torn what he knew of the gunrunner. "I didn't hear much, but they talked about guns and gold. Gatling guns."

"Gold," mumbled Johnny over a mouthful of army biscuit. "That reminds me." He dug into a pocket of his raggedy breeches and brandished a gold double eagle.

"Where did you get that?" asked Torn.

"An old Mexican sheepherder named Emiliano. Lives a few miles out of Eagle Pass. Used to come by the store every now and then, whenever he had a little money. He has a taste for licorice sticks. He come in the day Santiago hit. I asked him where he got this, and he admitted Santiago had given it to him. Santiago rode through Emiliano's place on his way to Eagle Pass. His men killed Emiliano's sheepdog, and Santiago paid him off with this double eagle."

"My God!" breathed Chapman. "The railroad payroll. It must be."

"What about it?" asked Torn.

"About ten days ago the Texas Pacific put fifty thousand dollars into the Eagle Pass bank for safekeeping. Payroll money. I commanded the detail escorting the payroll from Brownsville. Santiago must have it now. That's what he's using to buy those guns from Yarrow."

"Flynn asked about the bank, remember? And according to Alvarez, Flynn had at least one sack of gold double eagles in his floor safe the very morning Santiago hit Eagle Pass."

"What are you trying to say?"

Torn smiled. "It makes sense. My guess is that somehow Flynn got his hands on that payroll long before Santiago crossed the Rio Grande. He paid Santiago to abduct Meg Slaughter with most of it. Kept some for himself, of course. Naturally everybody would assume Santiago robbed the bank during the raid. In fact, the bank had already been robbed."

"I never heard about no bank robbery," said Johnny.

"I don't mean masked men making smoke," said Torn.

"You mean an inside job," said Chapman, suddenly comprehending.

"Possible?" asked Torn.

Chapman nodded grimly. "I think you might have hit the nail on the head, Judge. I never did trust Farraday —he's the bank president. He and Flynn go way back."

"Pretty clever plan Flynn cooked up," said Torn.

"So we know. Or think we do. But what good does it do us?"

"If we can take that gold back with us, you'll find out."

"I don't give a damn about the gold," said Chapman, obstinate. "It's Meg I'm worried about. And I think I know how we can get her away from Santiago."

"We trade the guns to Santiago in exchange for Meg."

Chapman nodded.

"How many men do you figure this Darby Yarrow has with him?" asked Torn.

"Can't say. I counted four with him when he paid his call on Santiago. There'll be more, watching the guns. But one thing's certain: he won't have as many as ride with Santiago."

"So all we've got to do is find the place Yarrow is hiding his merchandise."

"He fancies himself a gentleman. Lives high on the hog. Travels in style—a custom-made coach. There's only one road out of Tres Cruces. Heads east into rough country. Canyons and breaks, plenty of hideouts."

"If we ride hard we might be able to catch this Englishman," said Torn.

"Doesn't bother you, giving Santiago those Gatling guns?"

"We don't have 'em yet."

"You know what I mean."

"It doesn't bother me giving them to him," said Torn, turning for the picket line. "I didn't say anything about letting him keep them."

CHAPTER 24

IT WAS CODI WHO KILLED THE HORSE.

He used Johnny Rand's Sharps. The breechloader was a big-bore, long-range gun, the kind hide hunters used to bring down buffalo. His shot wasn't really all that long—he was hidden in the rocks about fifty yards above the road—but the Sharps was more accurate than his army-issue carbine. It also had a stronger punch, and the offside wheeler was a big animal.

It was dark, but that didn't hinder Codi much. He could see like a cat in the night, and Darby Yarrow's coach and its six-horse hitch were sharply delineated shapes against the pale dust of the road.

The wheeler dropped in its traces as the deep-throated boom of the Sharps echoed off the shale slopes and spires of the canyon Torn had picked for the ambush. The gunrunner's custom-made coach wasn't moving very fast; the team was straining up a fairly steep gradient. The dead horse acted like an anchor, bringing the coach to a jarring stop. The rest of the hitch started acting up, lurching in their traces, but neither team nor coach was going anywhere until the carcass of the offside wheeler had been cut out of harness.

Codi flipped the breechloader's leaf-sight down and proceeded down the slope with the surefooted agility of a mountain goat. He gave Torn silent kudos. The man in black was almost as good as an Apache in the fine art of ambushing.

Torn had picked Codi because the scout was the best shot of them all—a fact amply demonstrated during the fight with the Coronado men at the river, when Codi had made every bullet count from the rim of the bluff. He had made it clear to the Apache that it was one of the wheelers that had to be put down, and stressed the point that it should be done while the coach was on a slow upgrade haul. Had Codi shot one of the leaders while the coach was rolling at a rapid clip, there would have been a wreck, for certain.

And if the second half of Torn's plan was to work, they needed Darby Yarrow's fancified Abbot & Downing in one piece.

The gunrunner's men began firing upslope. Codi heard bullets slap rock to left and right, but he didn't miss a stride. The *Nakai-Ye* were shooting blind.

Thirty feet back down the road from the spot where the coach had come to an abrupt stop, Torn emerged from a clump of boulders and gave a shout.

One of the two mounted escorts reined his horse sharply and fired at the sound of Torn's voice. His shot went wide. Looking up the grade, Torn could clearly see the horseman's silhouette against a star-bright sky.

He had the added advantage of shooting at the other's muzzle flash. Torn fired twice. Both bullets found their marks, and the rider was dead before he hit the ground.

Breaking into a run, Torn made for the coach. The second outrider appeared from the other side of the Abbot & Downing. He could just barely make Torn out against the pale dust of the narrow road, and started shooting. Torn jumped sideways, crouching, and answered with the Colt Peacemaker. For a moment they traded lead. Torn moved after every shot. He had some trouble hitting his target because he couldn't predict the antics of his adversary's horse. But the last bullet in the Colt's cylinder struck home. The rider cried out and fell sideways out of the saddle.

Chapman and Johnny were coming hell-for-leather down the road, straight at the coach on thundering horses. They blazed away at the box, where Yarrow's other two men were located. One of the two pitched forward, shot through the throat, landing on the dead wheeler. The second man, the driver, decided it was time to make tracks. He hurled himself off the coach, landed in a graceless stumble and roll, picked himself up, and started running.

He didn't get far. Codi appeared suddenly in his path. The Mexican uttered a strangled cry of sheer terror at sight of the Apache. Codi hit him in the crotch with the stock of the Sharps. The driver jackknifed, and the scout laid the breechloader's barrel across his skull, none too gently. The driver collapsed. Drawing his knife, Codi straddled the unconscious man, bent on taking his scalp.

"No!" snapped Torn.

Codi looked up, and Torn could almost see the hate

blazing in the Apache's eyes. Of course, that wasn't possible in the darkness, and yet . . .

"We need him alive," said Torn.

The scout stepped away from the driver. Torn turned his attention to the coach.

"Darby Yarrow! Get your butt out here."

No sound issued from within the Abbot & Downing. Chapman and Johnny checked their horses, one on either side of the coach, and trained their guns on the doors.

"Don't make me come in after you, Yarrow," advised Torn.

The offside door swung open and the Englishman got out.

He looked at the bodies of his men with a studied air of indifference, casually swinging his walking stick. As Torn stepped cautiously closer Yarrow smiled affably. He appeared curious, but not the least bit afraid. The man, mused Torn, was either a very fine actor or had ice water in his veins.

"I don't believe I know you, old boy," drawled the gunrunner.

"No. I'm happy to say we haven't met until now."

Yarrow glanced at Codi, Chapman, and Johnny Rand. The latter had come around from the other side of the coach.

"Might this be a holdup?"

"You could call it that," said Torn.

"You're doing business with Garza Santiago," said Chapman bluntly, cutting to the quick. "We're going to take over your end of the deal."

"Indeed? And what makes you think Garza will do business with you gentlemen?"

"If he wants those Gatling guns, he will," replied Chapman.

"But you see, my good man, you'll never get those guns. Forty of my men are guarding them."

"Forty?" Torn smiled. "I have a hunch you're exaggerating."

The Englishman shrugged. "Don't say I didn't warn you. So what becomes of me, pray tell?"

"You've got one chance," said Torn. "Take your men —however many there really are—and ride back to Veracruz."

"Leaving the merchandise in your possession, I presume."

"You presume right."

"I'm awfully sorry, but I really couldn't oblige. I sincerely would like to avert bloodshed—I abhor violence, you know."

"A gunrunner who dislikes violence," said Chapman, sarcastic.

"But I have my reputation to consider," continued Yarrow. "Reputation means a great deal down here. These people put a lot of stock in that sort of thing. I'm afraid you blokes will have to try to take those guns by force. I'd wager you'll die trying."

"Go ahead, Judge," said Chapman. "Kill him. He's no use to us."

Torn raised the Colt Peacemaker.

Yarrow stopped smiling. He jumped back, twisting the handle of the walking stick just so. The cane separated at the ferrule, and the Englishman brandished the concealed rapier. He lunged at Torn, and the razor-sharp blade sliced through Torn's coat and shirt and would have pierced his chest if he hadn't been endowed with such superlative reflexes. He felt a sharp lancing pain as the rapier grazed one of his ribs. The barrel of his Colt came down hard on Yarrow's hand, knocking the rapier out of the gunrunner's grasp, and a half second later his left fist connected solidly with Yarrow's face. The Englishman and the rapier hit the ground at the same time.

It had been a close call; Torn knew it, and it made his blood boil. He hauled Yarrow to his feet and slammed him against the cambered side of the coach. Then he put the Colt to Yarrow's forehead and thumbed back the hammer.

"Say good-bye, old chap," growled Torn.

"No!" screamed Yarrow.

Torn pulled the trigger.

Yarrow's whole body, from hairline to heel, spasmed.

The hammer fell on an empty chamber.

"Damn," breathed Torn. "I forgot to reload."

He holstered the Colt, reached under his frock coat, and drew the saber-knife from its shoulder rig. "Instead of blowing your head off, Mr. Yarrow," he said with a cold smile, "I'll have to cut it off."

Yarrow's knees had turned to jelly. Only the fact that Torn had him pinned to the side of the coach kept him from collapsing. He had soiled himself, and his eyes were wet.

Torn knew he had broken the man.

"I'll do what you want," whispered Yarrow. "For the love of God don't kill me. You can have the Gatlings. Just don't . . ."

Torn let go of him and stepped back.

Yarrow sat down hard and covered his face with his hands.

"You and Johnny go fetch the rest of our horses," Torn told Chapman.

The lieutenant nodded, urged his mount into a canter up the road. Riding alongside, Johnny threw a glance over his shoulder.

"That Judge Torn is one cold-blooded customer," said the youngster.

"Smart, too," replied Chapman. "He knew damned good and well his gun was empty when he pulled the trigger."

CHAPTER 25

AT FIRST LIGHT, OCHOA BROUGHT THE NEWS TO SANTIAGO.

"Garza! The Englishman comes back."

Santiago snapped wide awake. He lay in the bed that had once belonged to the Tres Cruces alcalde, Clara beside him.

"What?"

"The Englishman is back."

"Something's wrong," growled Santiago. He rolled out of bed and dressed quickly. Ochoa's eyes strayed to the woman. Her wrists were tied to one of the bedposts. The rumpled covers did not hide her nakedness. Ochoa tried not to look too hard in Santiago's presence, but it wasn't easy to ignore her. She was very pretty, even though her left eye was swollen almost shut. There were some unsightly bruises on her face and shoulders as well.

"Put her with the other woman," snapped Santiago, on his way out.

Stepping out of the alcalde's house, Garza looked up the street in the direction of the square. Yarrow's coach was trundling down the *calle,* thoroughbraces creaking, trace chains jangling.

The bandit leader's eyes narrowed suspiciously. There was only one man in the Abbot & Downing's box —the reinsman. No outriders. And only four horses in the hitch.

Santiago cast a quick look around. Tres Cruces was quiet. Two of his men stood near the low adobe wall encircling the alcalde's house, watching the coach draw near. Another staggered out of a casa across the street, only to trip and fall over one of his *compudres,* who was passed out in the doorway. One of many, mused Santiago sourly, who were sleeping off last night's excesses.

The coach's driver climbed the reins that were threaded through his fingers and brought the Abbot & Downing to a halt beyond the wall.

Torn stepped out.

Santiago's eyes widened in surprise. "You!"

Torn walked through the gate like he owned the place, his Winchester 44/40 shoulder-racked.

The two bandits who had been loitering near the wall flicked their cigarettes away and moved to block Torn's passage, reaching for their pistols.

"No!" barked Santiago. "Leave him alone."

The *bandoleros* stepped aside, scowling fiercely at Torn. Torn ignored them and walked straight up to Santiago.

"Where is the Englishman?" asked Garza.

"Long gone."

"You have come for the girl. I knew you would. You bring my knife?"

Torn held his frock coat open, allowing Santiago a glimpse of the saber-knife held tight against his rib cage in its shoulder harness. "You're right," he said. "I've come for Meg Slaughter. I know all about your deal with Flynn. And I have those Gatling guns. You know, the ones you think will make you the new president of Mexico. You can have them, in exchange for Meg."

"She is your woman, hombre?"

"Her father is a friend."

Santiago grunted, looked beyond Torn at the two *garcistas*. "Bring me that man," he said, pointing at the driver.

The reinsman, who had the look of someone who wished fervently to be elsewhere, was hustled unceremoniously into Garza's presence.

"Tell me what happened," said Santiago.

The driver's voice was shaky. "This man and some others, they ambush us. Only Señor Yarrow and I survive."

"How many others?"

"I saw three more. One Apache. They shot one of the team to stop the coach in a canyon not far from here."

Santiago nodded. That explained why two of the horses were missing from the hitch. Since they had not been able to replace the dead animal with another trained to the trace, a second horse had been taken out of harness to maintain the balance of the hitch.

"This one," said Yarrow's driver, gesturing at Torn, "said he would let the Apache kill me slow if I did not do what he told me."

Santiago turned to Torn. "Why do you come in the Englishman's coach?"

"How far would I have gotten otherwise?"

"And so you make this man bring you."

"It looked better."

Santiago chuckled. It wasn't a pleasant sound, from Torn's perspective. "I will make a deal with you, gringo. You give me the Gatling guns and I will let you and your three *compadres* live. And you will give me my knife, too."

"I'm not leaving without Meg Slaughter."

"Ah. *Mucho hombre,* eh? We will see. You want to know what I think? I think you will tell me where the guns are. You will beg me to let you before this day is out. And then, when I know what I want to know, I will take pity on you and let you die. Take him, hombres!"

Torn whirled, sweeping the Winchester down off his shoulder. The rifle's barrel caught one of the bandits across the jaw, breaking bone. The blow hurled the man sideways, into the path of his *compañero*. Torn continued to spin, turning to face Santiago once more, bringing the Winchester down to hip level, ready to fire, hoping he hadn't bent the barrel.

But he wasn't quite quick enough.

Santiago's pistol caught him on the temple. A brief explosion of nauseating pain preceded an unending fall into the black bottomless pit of oblivion.

CHAPTER 26

TORN WAS STRUNG UP LIKE A SIDE OF BEEF IN THE *RAMADA di herrero,* the shed of the village blacksmith, not far from the alcalde's house. The hemp bindings that suspended him from the roof's mesquite poles cut into his raw and bleeding wrists. His toes dangled inches from the hardpack. They had removed his coat and shirt and boots. From neck to waist his back was a bloody mass of long, seeping gashes, and his face was battered into a misshapen mask of dried black blood and red welts.

A few feet away, Yarrow's driver also hung from the roof poles. He, too, was stripped to the waist. Blood leaked out of both corners of his mouth and dribbled down onto his chest. Otherwise he appeared undamaged. One of the bandits who had been torturing Torn had threatened the blubbering reinsman with the latigo strap he had been using as a whip. The driver had screamed hoarsely, bitten his tongue almost in two, and fainted. Disappointed, the bandit had turned his attention back to Torn. The gringo was proving to be a much more durable victim.

"Tell us where the guns are," growled the bandit, shaking the bloody latigo strap in front of Torn's face.

"Go to hell," croaked Torn.

The *garcista* went to work with sadistic pleasure. Torn's body convulsed in a rigid arch as the leather sliced his flesh. But he made no sound. He wasn't going to give the bastard the satisfaction of hearing him scream.

The bandit with the whip tired himself out laying Torn's back open. He had lost count of the strokes. His bare chest, crossed with bandoliers, was splattered with Torn's blood and his own sweat. More blood, more sweat streaked his coarse face. Every time he brought the wide leather strap back for another blow, a spray of blood came off it.

The second *garcista* sweated over red-hot coals, working leathern bellows on the stone lip of the blacksmith's forge. A pair of iron tongs lay with red-glowing tips in the heart of the fiery crucible.

At least two dozen other bandits had gathered to watch. They were making wagers among themselves concerning how long the gringo would hold out. He had held out a lot longer than any of them had thought possible. Those on the verge of losing shouted encouragement to the man with the whip.

But the latigo man was exhausted. He tossed his makeshift whip aside in disgust and stumbled to the low mud-brick wall encompassing the *ramada*. One of his *compañeros* handed him a wicker-encased jug of pulque, from which he had been drawing sustenance. He shook the jug, sloshing the contents, and frowned as he tried to judge the amount of sustenance that remained. He turned to his cohort.

"Hey, Pablo. I think I made a bad bet with you. I think the gringo will last longer than the pulque after all."

Pablo gave Torn a speculative glance. He did not like looking at the gringo. In fact, he did not much care for the whole business. He didn't mind robbing and killing —those were integral parts of his chosen profession— but he had decided he did not really have the stomach for torturing.

Privately Pablo was impressed by the prisoner's toughness. Carlos was a big, burly man who enjoyed inflicting pain, and did so with enthusiasm whenever the opportunity presented itself. That was why Santiago had chosen him. Pablo had been picked to assist Carlos because he had been the son of a blacksmith.

But for all Carlos's strength and enthusiasm, he had failed to break the Anglo. Pablo hailed from the seaside village of Pesca. Torn reminded him of the beach, and Carlos the storm-driven sea—a sea that hurled the sounding fury of its waves upon the beach. Again and again the waves pounded against the beach, but always fell back, exhausted; they left their mark, yet the beach remained, unyielding and inherently unchanged.

"Maybe you should try the other one," suggested Pablo, meaning Yarrow's driver.

"Bah, he does not know where this gringo hid the guns. If he had known, he would have told us at the very beginning."

Pablo nodded. *"Es verdad."* He sighed. "I don't think Garza expected to learn anything from him. But it was worth a try, I guess."

Having swallowed some pulque and caught his wind, Carlos rose and stepped across to Torn, standing in front of his victim and examining him the way a painter might critique his latest canvas. Then, cradling the jug in the crook of his thickly muscled arm, he took another long swig. Some of the fermented agave juice spilled down his chin and chest. He wiped his face with the back of his hand, smearing the blood and the sweat and the pulque together.

"Hey, hombre." Carlos was whispering, his leering face close to Torn's. "Are you still with us?"

Torn opened his left eye. His right was swollen shut. Carlos had gone wild with one of his blows, and the latigo strap had curled around Torn's head, laying open his cheek and injuring an eye.

Drawing his tongue over a parched upper lip, Torn hawked and spat into the bandit's face.

Carlos just laughed. It wasn't the reaction Torn had expected. In fact, it was more ominous than the beating he had been prepared to receive.

"You've got *huevos*, I'll give you that, gringo. But not for very much longer. We don't want you to make any more brave little gringos, to come down here and cause trouble for us."

Torn closed his good eye. He understood what Carlos was intending to do, but it did not move him to panic. Today he had learned that it was possible to live in a world of constant agony. He had become familiar with pain—had forgotten what it was like to be without it. There was no way to stop it, no way to avoid it, so he accepted it.

He was calm in the face of his tormentor's threat because he knew there was no hope. He had gambled and lost. Now he would die. But in a way he could die winning, by refusing to tell Santiago what he wanted to know.

It wasn't hard to die when you knew you were giving your life to save others.

In this case he was saving Chapman's life. Codi's and Johnny Rand's, too. And it was the last thing he could do to help Meg Slaughter, because as long as they were alive, there was a chance Chapman and the others could rescue her.

"Hey, hombre."

Torn opened the eye that still worked.

He saw Carlos first, and then the red-glowing tongs, held so close to his face that he flinched away from the searing heat.

Grinning, Carlos lowered the tongs.

27

When Santiago entered the room where Clara and Meg were being held, he found the Anglo woman ministering to the former, dabbing gingerly at Clara's bruises with a cloth that had been dipped in the brackish well water contained in a glazed clay bowl.

As Santiago approached, Meg hurled the cloth at him. "You're a sorry excuse for a man!"

Santiago held up the shoulder rig containing Torn's saber-knife. "Know who this belongs to, woman?"

Meg gasped. "Dear God in heaven. Clay . . ."

"The brave fool came to save you. He is learning the hard way that no woman is worth dying for."

Santiago touched Clara's cheek. She was sitting on the edge of the bed, wearing only her skirt. What remained of her tattered *camisa* lay across her lap. She made no effort to cover herself. Her expression was inscrutable as Santiago's hand traced the curve of her neck, brushed her shoulder, went lower. Clara's eyes were as dull and lifeless as a doll's.

"Leave her alone!" screamed Meg, launching herself at the bandit leader.

Santiago whirled and sent her sprawling with a brutal backhanded blow across the face.

The saber-knife rig fell to the floor.

"Maybe you want to take her place, eh?" Santiago leered, looming over Meg.

"You wouldn't dare," said Meg defiantly. "My father would hunt you down and kill you."

Santiago laughed. "Your father and I are going to do business together. How much do you think he will pay for you?"

"So you did take me for ransom. I thought so."

"Of course. But don't tell Flynn. He thinks he made a deal with me. He paid me well to kidnap you, and now he thinks he can use you to destroy your father. But Flynn should have known better than to trust me to carry out my end of the bargain. I have decided I will keep you, and to hell with Flynn. Your father will do what *I* want, not what Flynn wants."

Meg picked herself up off the floor, touched her lip, and looked at the blood on her fingers. "You bastard."

Santiago pretended to be shocked. "Is that any way for a lady to talk?"

"I'm no lady," said Meg—and kicked him as hard as she could between the legs.

With a grunting wheeze, Santiago doubled over, grabbing his crotch. Meg backed away. Growling like an animal, Santiago lunged at her. Grabbing the clay bowl, Meg swung it with all her might. The bowl shattered against Santiago's skull. Garza collapsed, out cold.

Hearing the commotion, the guard in the hall came through the door.

"Jefe?"

Clara moved, quick as thought. As the door began to swing open she scooped up the saber-knife, removed it from the sheath. When the *garcista* crossed the threshold, she was there to greet him. The bandit groped for the pistol at his side. Clara drove the saber-knife into his chest, turning the blade so that it could pass between his ribs. Cold steel plunged into the bandit's heart. He died instantly. Clara jerked the knife free and stepped back. Hot blood splattered her bare breasts as the dead man pitched forward.

Taking the bandit's pistol, Clara crossed the room to stand over Santiago.

"Don't kill him," said Meg.

Clara cocked the gun.

"Don't, please! I know how you must feel, but please, Clara, think!"

Squeezing her eyes tightly shut, Clara let the gun hammer down. "Tie him up," she said, her voice ragged. "We must be quick."

They used strips torn from the bedcover to bind Santiago's wrists. Then Clara slapped him until he came to. He opened his eyes to look straight down the barrel of a gun.

"You will do what I say," said Clara, "or you will never hear them call you *el presidente.*"

"Kill me now, whore."

"I would but for her." Clara nodded at Meg. "You will help us get out of here."

"You will die."

"You'll die with me."

Santiago showed no fear. "Very well. I have no choice."

* * *

It was Pablo who stopped Carlos from applying the red-hot tongs to Torn. "You will kill him," he argued. "And if he dies before telling us where the guns are hidden, you and I will find ourselves hanging here like him."

"Coward!" growled Carlos. "You don't have the stomach for it." He brushed the smaller man aside.

Torn summoned all the strength remaining in his punished body and, bringing his knees up, kicked out at Carlos with both feet, catching the man full in the chest and knocking him backward. Carlos collided with Pablo, who was scrambling to get out of the way, and both of them fell. The tongs landed on Carlos's leg, burning through his trousers and searing his flesh. He howled in pain. The crowd of bandits gathered around the *ramada* dissolved into laughter.

Humiliated, Carlos jumped up and proceeded to hammer his fists into Torn's midsection. Torn brought a knee up into the man's face, sent him reeling again. Some of the *garcistas* shouted approval; they admired Torn for his spirit. He was fighting as well as a man could in his position.

Carlos came back swinging, snarling like a mad dog.

"Stop!"

Every head turned. Staggering, winded, Carlos backed off and looked around, too.

It was Santiago, on horseback, his hands tied behind his back. Clara was astride another horse alongside his, holding a pistol to his head. She was a sight, wearing the bloody shirt of the guard she had killed. Torn's saber-knife rig was draped over the pommel of her saddle. Behind them was Meg Slaughter, also mounted, and leading a fourth horse.

The bandits were frozen a moment by this extraordinary sight. Their leader was being held at gunpoint by a woman! Then, almost in unison, they reached for their guns.

"I'll kill him!" screamed Clara. "Nobody moves!"

"Do as she says," commanded Santiago.

"Cut the gringo down," said Clara.

"Do it," said Santiago calmly.

Pablo drew his *belduque* from its belt sheath and sliced the rawhide. Torn fell to his knees, and Pablo cut the bindings from his wrists.

Sheer force of will got Torn to his feet. Head down, he locked his fevered gaze onto Carlos. He clenched and unclenched his hands as the blood began to circulate in them again. They were sticky with blood from his lacerated wrists.

Carlos stepped back, suddenly very much afraid of Torn. This man wasn't human. No ordinary human could have taken so much punishment. He had never known anyone to endure even half of what he had inflicted on Torn.

But Torn did not move on Carlos—instead he angled for the street, and the horse Meg was holding for him.

Grim, silent, the bandits parted to let him pass.

Torn crawled into the saddle.

"Oh, Clay," said Meg in a small voice, looking in horror upon his wounds. "You shouldn't have come for me."

"I had to."

"Father . . . is he . . . ?"

"He's fine. You'll soon be with him."

Torn urged his horse forward, reined up abreast of Santiago and Clara. The latter handed him his saber-knife and the saddlebags she had taken from the alcalde's house.

"What's this?" he asked.

"Gold." Clara didn't take her eyes off Santiago.

"You're coming with us," Torn told Garza. "Looks to me like this woman wants to shoot you so bad it hurts. So if I were you, I'd pray nobody takes a shot at one of us. That is, if you remember how to pray. Oh, and one more thing. You!" He pointed at Pablo. "Get over here."

Pablo complied.

"Give me your gun," said Torn.

Pablo glanced at Santiago. Santiago nodded, and Pablo surrendered his pistol to Torn.

"Let's go," said Torn. "Nice and easy."

They started off, keeping their horses to a walk. The bandits drifted out into the street behind them. They weren't sure what to do. Torn knew it was their fear of Santiago that held them at bay. No one wanted to be the man who fired the shot that put Santiago's life in jeopardy.

Because if, somehow, Santiago survived, that man would not.

Torn calculated it was maybe fifty yards to the edge of town, where the houses stopped and the road just turned into desert. Not far, but it seemed to take forever to cover the distance. They ran a gauntlet of more bandits, coming out of doorways and alleys to stand and watch their passage. A tense silence pervaded, broken only by the yapping of a dog and the squall of an infant child. Torn rode straight in the saddle, ignoring the pain, concentrating on the bandits along the road, watching for the first hostile move, and ready with a .45-caliber answer.

But it was Santiago who made the first move.

He slipped his booted foot out of the stirrup and kicked Clara's horse in the head. The animal snorted and reared. Clara toppled out of the saddle. The gun in her hand went off, but the bullet plowed into the hardpack. Santiago dug spur. His horse jumped like a jackrabbit. He rolled sideways out of the saddle. With his hands tied behind his back, he landed hard, but was on his feet in an instant and disappeared down an alley between two *chozas*.

The bandits started shooting.

Torn yelled, "Make a run for it!" As Meg galloped past he reached out a hand for Clara, who was picking herself up off the ground. Her horse had run off. She took Torn's hand. He kicked his own mount into a gallop and swung her up onto the cantle of the saddle. A bandit jumped out into the road in their path, blazing away. Torn shot him as they thundered past, chased by a swarm of hot lead.

A half mile out of town they checked their winded horses. Torn decided it was a certifiable miracle that none of them had been hit. He looked back toward Tres Cruces, saw the dust that told him all he needed to know.

"They're coming," he said.

"Leave me," Clara said in Spanish. "The horse won't make it carrying double."

Meg translated for Torn's benefit. He shook his head.

"We'll make it. We don't have far to go."

He could hear the thunder of a hundred horses at the gallop, faint but ominous. The sound sent a chill down his spine. It was the sound of his dream. He kicked his reluctant mount into motion and headed east across the malpais, Meg Slaughter riding beside him.

CHAPTER 28

THE CHASE ENDED IN THE CANYON NOT FAR FROM THE SPOT where Torn, Chapman, and the others had bushwhacked the British gunrunner, Darby Yarrow.

It was there that the horse carrying Torn and Clara finally gave out. Its heart burst; its front legs buckled. The animal nose-dived into the dust with one last great sigh. Torn and Clara were thrown hard. Meg galloped past, reined up, and came back. Torn got up, helped Clara to her feet, and then went over to check the horse. He felt remorse. The game animal had carried them farther than he had expected. Not quite far enough, but almost.

The thunder that had followed them from Tres Cruces was much louder now, bouncing off the canyon slopes.

Torn took the saddlebags off the dead horse and handed them to Meg. "Chapman's waiting about a mile on up this canyon," he said tersely. "You two get going."

"What about you?"

"I'm going to buy you a little time."

"No, Clay! I can't let—"

"Get going!" snapped Torn. "No time to argue."

Tears in her eyes, Meg spoke to Clara in Spanish. Clara shook her head, and Torn didn't need to know the lingo to understand her reply.

"She says—" began Meg.

"I don't need her to look after." Torn picked Clara up bodily and threw her across the bow of Meg's saddle. The horse snorted, sidestepping. Meg grabbed hold of Clara as Torn slapped the horse hard on the rump. It galloped up-canyon—just as Santiago and his men appeared two hundred yards down-canyon.

As soon as they saw Torn, they started shooting.

Torn dived behind the carcass of the dead horse. He didn't return fire immediately. Keeping his head down, he checked the loads in the pistol. Six beans in the cylinder. He resolved to wait until they were right up on him. With any luck, Santiago would be in the lead. If he could take Garza with him to the grave, then that would be something worthwhile to go out on.

Once, he looked behind him, and was relieved to see that Meg and Clara had disappeared around a dogleg bend in the canyon. He prayed they would reach Chapman. Perhaps then they'd stand a chance.

And he prayed that wherever she was, Melony Hancock was safe and sound.

He'd had a hunch all along that he would die without knowing what had become of her.

The ground shook beneath him. The thunder was loud in his ears. He felt the impact of bullets striking the dead horse. Bullets whined off rocks. Bullets kicked up dust in the road all around him. He was right in the middle of a hot lead hailstorm.

Then he heard the stuttering cough of a Gatling gun.

He rolled over on his back and looked up-canyon. One of the wagons Yarrow had used to transport his shipment from Veracruz was careening around the bend. Johnny Rand was handling the two horses in the hitch. Chapman was operating the Gatling, which was set up in the bed of the wagon, lashed down with rope. Meg stood in the back of the wagon alongside the lieutenant, handing him fresh magazines. Sunlight flashed off the ten revolving barrels of the gun, and off a steady stream of ejected shell casings. Johnny was bending low, because the Gatling was spewing lead at the rate of four hundred rounds a minute just above and behind his head. Clara was riding the horse she and Meg had shared a moment before, keeping up with the wagon and making smoke with a pistol.

The Gatling's effect on the bandits, bunched together in the narrow canyon, was devastating. Men and horses went down in big bloody batches. Some turned and ran. Others tried to escape by scaling the steep rocky slopes of the canyon. Those made of sterner stuff pressed forward. Torn shot one *garcista* out of the saddle as the bandit's horse raced by. He sent three more rounds into the melee of dust and death.

Behind him, Johnny climbed the leathers and brought the wagon to a skittering sideways halt. He grabbed up a Spencer carbine and jumped out of the box. Bullets caught him in midair, and he sprawled in the road, unmoving. Chapman kept cranking the Gatling gun and Meg kept changing out the magazines.

Torn got up and headed for the wagon at a run. Swirling dust obscured his vision. Too late, he heard the horse bearing down on him from behind. He was turning when Garza Santiago launched himself out of the saddle and carried Torn to the ground. Torn lost his grip on the pistol. He rolled, came up in a crouch, reached for the saber-knife rig stuck in his belt. Santiago was already on his feet. Grinning like a wolf, the bandit leader aimed his gun at Torn. It was Torn's own Colt Peacemaker.

Though he knew he stood no chance, Torn drew the saber-knife from its sheath and charged forward.

At least, he thought, I won't die with a bullet in the back.

The Colt's hammer fell on an empty chamber.

Santiago's grin vanished as Torn plowed into him. He knocked Garza to the ground, fell on top of him, and plunged the saber-knife into the bandit leader's midsection.

"Viva Santiago," said Torn through clenched teeth.

Santiago's rigid body spasmed once and then went limp.

The Gatling gun fell silent. Sporadic gunfire quickly died out, and then the only sounds were those made by dying men and horses.

Torn got to his feet, the Colt in one hand, the bloody saber-knife in the other, and moved to the wagon. Chapman and Meg were gathered around Johnny Rand.

"Santiago . . ." gasped Johnny through a blood-tinged froth.

"Done for," said Torn.

"Flynn . . . I wish . . ."

Torn shook his head. Even on the brink of death the boy wouldn't let go of revenge.

"I'll take care of Flynn," he promised.

Meg sobbed and stumbled away. She knew there

was no hope for Johnny and couldn't bear to watch. Chapman went after her.

Johnny seemed to be looking right through Torn at something only he could see. A smile wrenched the corner of his mouth.

"Hello, Pa . . ." he breathed.

It was his last breath.

The dust was beginning to settle, and Torn stood there a moment, gazing down-canyon at the carnage. He figured the Gatling gun had accounted for forty or fifty *bandoleros* in a matter of minutes. It had happened so quickly. So much death in so short a time—so much that Torn, who had seen too much killing, was shocked. In places the corpses were heaped in piles. A few riderless horses stood among the dead, heads down, as though they, too, were affected by the terrible scene.

What was left of Santiago's bandit army was long gone.

Chapman's anguished shout captured Torn's attention. He saw the lieutenant running up the canyon road and followed.

Clara was kneeling next to Codi's body. The Apache scout lay across the corpse of a *garcista*. His lifeless hand still gripped the knife buried in the bandit's side. And the bandit still held the gun, which, Torn surmised, had taken Codi's life.

"Es muerte," said Clara. Recognizing the grief that twisted Chapman's features, she spoke to him a moment in Spanish. Chapman nodded and turned away.

"What did she say?" asked Torn.

"Codi saved her life. She was out of ammunition. Her horse threw her. This bandit was all set to finish her when Codi came down out of the rocks. He was up yonder, picking them off with a long gun." Chapman drew a ragged breath. "Ironic, isn't it? Codi died to save the life of a *Nakai-Ye*."

"We're lucky you came along when you did."

"You were overdue. So we rigged one of the Gatlings up in the wagon and headed for Tres Cruces. Didn't know what else to do. I sure wasn't going to sit there till Christmas, waiting for you. We spotted the dust. Codi went on ahead, up to the rimrock, to see if he could get a look." Chapman shook his head. "He was a good friend, Judge. And a damn fine scout."

"One of the best," said Torn.

CHAPTER 29

ONE WEEK LATER . . .

Aloysius Flynn woke with a start.

At first he wasn't sure what had awakened him. The hacienda was still. It was the middle of the night. Through the open window of his second-story bedroom, Flynn could hear the chorus of bullfrogs down by the river.

He rose and crossed to the window in his nightshirt. The bunkhouses and *ranchito* were dark and quiet. Not a breath of wind stirred the curtains on the window, and Flynn wiped the perspiration from his furrowed brow with the back of his hand. Maybe, he thought, it was the relentless heat that had disturbed his sleep. Yes, that had to be it.

Halfway back to bed, he froze, hearing the creak of a floorboard in the hallway outside.

Someone else was in the house.

Flynn's first thought was of the sentries posted round-the-clock on the roof above. How had the intruder managed to get inside without being seen? Flynn was more angry than afraid. He swore to himself that if he learned the lookouts were sleeping on the job he would have them strung up by their thumbs.

Grabbing up the Remington Navy that lay on a table beside the bed, Flynn threw open the bedroom door and charged out into the hallway.

He figured the intruder was one of his own vaqueros, looking for something of value to steal before making dust for parts unknown. It had happened before. He didn't trust Mexicans. He gave them work and a fair wage and sometimes they still stole from him. Ungrateful wretches. It was so hard to get good help on the Bloody Border.

The upstairs hall was dark and empty.

Flynn's nape hair crawled as he heard the telltale creak on the stairs at the end of the hall.

"Who is that?" he bellowed.

No answer.

Flynn swallowed the lump in his throat. He went back into the bedroom, lighted a lamp, and ventured out into the hall again. He paused a moment, listening hard, but heard nothing more. Going to the top of the staircase, he saw lamplight leaking under the doors to the front parlor downstairs.

The room where the floor safe was located.

Forgetting his fear, Flynn pounded down the stairs and barged into the room, finger on the trigger.

He was scarcely through the door when Torn hit him at the base of the skull with the barrel of the Colt Peacemaker—a carefully measured blow. Flynn crumpled. The Remington skittered across the floor. The Irishman groaned and dry-heaved. Holstering the Colt,

Torn picked the half-conscious man up and deposited him in a velvet-upholstered wing chair. Flynn lolled forward and Torn pushed him back. Then he turned to retrieve the Remington, slipping it under his belt, and moved on to the sideboard. He poured himself a shot glass full of bourbon, downed it, and refilled the glass. This he carried back to Flynn. Splashed the bourbon in the rancher's face.

Sputtering, Flynn regained his senses. He focused on Torn's bruised and battered face and gasped in horror.

"Mother Mary!"

"Try again."

"You! But . . . but I thought you . . ."

"You should have run, Flynn. As far and as fast as you could."

"I figured you for dead. They told me Chapman had deserted. When you crossed over into Mexico, I thought you were going after Santiago. I didn't think you'd stand a chance. . . ."

"Santiago's dead. And there's not much left of his so-called army, either."

Flynn turned quite pale.

"Meg Slaughter's safe," said Torn.

The rancher's blunt fingers dug into the rich fabric on the arms of the chair.

"And you," said Torn, "you're finished. I know everything. All about the Texas Pacific payroll. The plan to abduct Meg. How you sent Frank Robles and his crew out to be butchered by Santiago, just to make it look as though you'd suffered at the hands of the *garcistas,* along with everyone else."

"No one will believe you," said Flynn, mustering half-baked bluster.

"Don't be too sure. I've got most of the payroll. I've come here for the rest."

"I don't have—"

"Don't lie to me," growled Torn.

His mind racing, Flynn took a deep, ragged breath. "But everyone thinks Santiago took the payroll from the bank during the raid. You can't tie me to that. You can't tie me to anything. My hands are clean."

"Wrong. Santiago was throwing those double eagles around *before* the raid. And you had some of them in your floor safe the same morning the bandits were shooting up Eagle Pass."

Flynn licked his lips. Sweat trickled down his forehead and into his eyes.

"Alvarez told you that. And Alvarez is dead."

"Farraday isn't. What do you want to bet I can make him talk?"

"Okay." Flynn's tone was one of resignation. "Okay, you win. Look, Torn, I'll give you everything in the safe. About ten thousand dollars. Take it for yourself. Take the whole flamin' payroll for yourself. All I ask is a fast horse and one hour's head start."

"You're coming with me back to Eagle Pass. Now get the rest of that payroll."

Flynn stood and crossed the room. Kneeling, he threw back one of the Mexican rugs. He glanced over his shoulder to confirm that Torn hadn't moved—was still standing over by the chair. Grabbing an iron ring that rested flat in a recess, Flynn lifted a small trapdoor. He reached down to the safe, worked the combination dial, opened the heavy steel door.

The hideout, a Smith & Wesson Pocket .32, lay atop the five sacks filled with gold double eagles.

Flynn grabbed the gun, stood, and turned.

He thought Torn was still across the room.

He was wrong.

Torn had moved, and Flynn hadn't heard a sound. In

fact, Torn was standing so close he was able to reach out and wrench the hideout from Flynn's grasp. At the same time he drove the saber-knife to the hilt into Flynn just below the sternum.

Flynn's mouth gaped open. His eyes bulged as fifteen inches of cold steel ripped through him.

"Alvarez told me about the gun, too," said Torn, and twisted the blade before pulling it free.

Vomiting blood, Flynn fell to his knees, clutching at the wound. He stared at the blood on his hands before falling forward on his face. He twitched once more. Torn heard the death rattle.

Collecting the sacks of double eagles, he slipped away from the hacienda. The lookouts hadn't seen him come, and they didn't see him go. He moved through the night quiet as a shadow. Quiet as an Apache.

Chapman and Meg were waiting for him in the trees down by the river.

"Where's Flynn?" asked Chapman.

"Dead."

"Well," said Chapman. He was too miserable to say anything else.

"He wouldn't have admitted to anything," said Torn.

"So what do we do now?" asked Meg.

"I live the rest of my life looking over my shoulder," said Chapman woodenly. "Torn will take you home."

"No," breathed Meg, tears glistening in her eyes. She looked at Torn. "Please . . ."

"Is there a place near here where you can hole up for a day or two, Lieutenant?" asked Torn.

Chapman thought it over. "Remember Johnny Rand mentioned an old sheepherder named Emiliano? I know him. He has a place a few miles from Camp Warren. . . ."

Torn nodded. "Good enough. I'll find it. You wait for me there."

"Why? Where are you going?"

"I'm taking the payroll back. And I plan to have a talk with the bank president, Farraday. Also Colonel Dalworth."

"It won't do any good," muttered Chapman.

"Just wait for me," said Torn curtly. He mounted up, glanced at Meg.

"I'll wait with Oliver," she said. "It may be all the time we have to spend together."

Again Torn nodded. Meg Slaughter had made her decision. Strangely her words did not dismay him. He had made his own decision. He wasn't sure when or where he'd made it, but he knew it was the right one.

Without another word he rode away.

CHAPTER 30

Two days later Torn arrived at Emiliano's place, the remote hut deep in the scrub oak and sagebrush *brasada*. Chapman and Meg were there, but the old Mexican was off looking after his sheep.

"Your father's doing fine," he told Meg, first thing. "He still can't get around much. I told him you'd be home today."

"I must go see him," she told Chapman, putting her hand on the lieutenant's arm.

Chapman nodded, a stricken look on his face. "You should have gone back with Torn."

"But I wanted to spend some time with you, Oliver."

Chapman didn't say anything.

"I'll make some coffee," said Meg in a small voice, and went inside the hut.

Torn dismounted, moving stiffly. His wounds were still hurting him. Leading his horse to the well, he drew some water and let the animal drink. Chapman followed him.

"You'll see her home, won't you?" asked the lieutenant. "And . . . and I suppose you'll take good care of her, too."

Torn hauled off and hit him.

Chapman ended up on his butt, rubbing his jaw. "What did you do that for?"

"Trying to knock some sense into you. By God, Chapman, there aren't many things in this life worth holding on to, and here you are trying to throw one of them away."

"What are you talking about?"

"I'm talking about a woman who loves you. If you're smart, you'll do whatever it takes to keep her. If you really love her."

"Of course I do. So do you."

"No," said Torn. "I thought I could learn to. But that's not how it works. I love someone else. Always will."

Chapman picked himself up, brushed off the seat of his pants. "But I can't ask her to share the life of a deserter."

"Stow it," said Torn, exasperated. "You're ordered to report to Camp Warren for duty tomorrow."

Chapman was thunderstruck. "You're pulling my leg."

"I had a long talk with Colonel Dalworth. It so happens that while we were away they pushed through that Hot Trail Treaty with Mexico. You're a big hero for putting an end to Garza Santiago. Even the colonel comes out of this looking pretty good. He still has to explain to a board of inquiry why he got caught flat-footed when Santiago came across the river, but this might just salvage his career."

"I don't follow you."

"Officially he sent you to Mexico, Chapman. A special mission. You and Codi. It was all Dalworth's idea. You savvy? You might even get a medal. Codi, too."

Chapman was too stunned to answer.

"Farraday, the bank president, talked. The Texas Pacific is right glad to get its payroll back. Everybody's happy with the way things turned out. The only time Dalworth got cranky was when I told him we gave those Gatling guns to the people of Tres Cruces. I also told him you taught them how to use the Gatlings that week I was healing up."

"Well," said Chapman, "I have a feeling those Tres Cruces folks won't have to worry about bandits anymore."

"Maybe." Torn sounded dubious.

He climbed back into the saddle.

"Leaving so soon? Meg will want to say good-bye."

Torn glanced at the hut with hooded eyes, then turned his gaze to distant heat shimmer, seeking the elusive malpais horizon. "I've got a lot of ground to cover."

"Going back to being a federal judge?"

"I never did get around to putting my resignation in writing."

Chapman held out a hand. "I never really liked you, Torn, I admit. But . . . well, thanks."

Torn shook the lieutenant's hand. "That's all right, Chapman. I never liked you, either."

He kicked the horse into a canter and did not look back. He was on the right track again, and knew it. Before the day was done, he'd put a lot of miles behind him. Tonight he would sleep well, and wake to the promise of a new day.

Tomorrow might be the day he found Melony.

If not, maybe the day after.

At least he could count on sleeping well. He was confident he would never have that nightmare again. And that was just as well, because he didn't want to see the face of the fourth shadow rider.

Even though he knew perfectly well who that fourth rider was.

HarperPaperbacks *By Mail*

If you like Westerns, you'll love these...

8 WESTERN CLASSICS

THE GLORY TRAIL
by *Mike Blakely*... Few men have a bigger dream than Texas Ranger Lawnce McCrary to make Texas a land of peace.

DIRK'S RUN
by *Paul Garrisen*... Dirk wasn't running from danger—he was riding toward death

VENDETTA GOLD
by *Mike Blakely*... author of "The Glory Trail"—Before Roy Huckaby can find the hidden treasure, he must first help settle a bloody family land war

TEXAS DRIVE by *Bill Dugan*... In the lawless west, you either pack a gun—or die!

DIRK'S REVENGE
by *Paul Garrisen*... Dirk was a gun for hire—and a man marked for death.

SPIRIT'S GOLD
by *Stuart Dillon*... He'll risk his life to find a beautiful woman's hidden fortune in gold.

GUN PLAY AT CROSS CREEK by *Bill Dugan*... Morgan Atwater can't run from the past—he has to settle in blood!

DUEL ON THE MESA
by *Bill Dugan*... After his family is massacred, Dalton Chance wants nothing except Indian blood!

...from today's best selling Western authors. Authors like Mike Blakely, Paul Garrisen, Bill Dugan, Stuart Dillon.

Visa and MasterCard holders—call
1-800-562-6182 for fastest service!

MAIL TO:
Harper Paperbacks, 120 Brighton Road
PO Box 5069, Clifton, NJ 07015-5069

Yes, please send me the Western Classics I have checked:
[ ] The Glory Trail (0-06-100013-2) $3.50
[ ] Dirk's Run (0-06-100035-3) $3.50
[ ] Vendetta Gold (0-06-100014-0) $3.50
[ ] Texas Drive (0-06-100032-9) $3.50
[ ] Dirk's Revenge (0-06-100035-3) $3.50
[ ] Spirit's Gold (0-06-100054-X) $3.95
[ ] Gun Play at Cross Creek (0-06-100079-5) . $3.50
[ ] Duel at The Mesa (0-06-100033-7) $3.50

SUBTOTAL . . . . $_____

POSTAGE AND HANDLING* . . . . $_____

SALES TAX (NJ, NY, PA residents) . . . . . . $_____

                  TOTAL: $_____
(Remit in US funds, do not send cash)

Name_____

Address_____

City_____

State_____ Zip_____

Allow up to 6 weeks delivery
Prices subject to change

*Add $1 postage, handling for up to 3 books
FREE postage/handling if you buy 4 or more.

HP-004

If you enjoyed the Zane Grey book you have just read...

GET THESE 8 GREAT

Harper Paperbacks brings you Zane Grey,

THE RAINBOW TRAIL. Shefford rides a perilous trail to a small stone house near Red Lake, where a new enemy awaits him—and an Indian girl leads him on a dangerous adventure toward Paradise Valley and his explosive destiny.

THE DUDE RANGER. Greenhorn Ernest Selby inherits a sprawling Arizona ranch that's in big trouble. Pitted against the crooked ranch manager and his ruthless band of outlaws, Selby is sure bullets will fly....

THE BORDER LEGION. Roving outlaws led by the notorious Kells kidnap an innocent young bride and hold her in their frightening grasp. Thus begins a wave of crime that could be stopped only by a member of their own vicious legion of death.

THE MAN OF THE FOREST. Milt Dale wanders alone amid the timbered ridges and dark forests of the White Mountains. One night, he stumbles upon a frightening plot that drives him from his beloved wilderness with a dire warning and an inspiring message.

THE LOST WAGON TRAIN. Tough Civil War survivor Stephen Latch will never be the same again. Emerged from the bloodshed a bitter man, a brigand with a ready gun, he joins a raging Indian chief on a mission of terrifying revenge—to massacre a pioneer train of 160 wagons. But fate has a big surprise!

WILDFIRE. Wildfire is a legend, a fiery red stallion who is captured and broken by horse trainer Lin Stone. A glorious beast, a miracle, Wildfire is also a curse—a horse who could run like the wind and who could also spill the blood of those who love him most.

HarperPaperbacks *By Mail*

ZANE GREY WESTERNS

the greatest chronicler of the American West!

SUNSET PASS. Six years ago Trueman Rock killed a man in Wagontongue. Now he's back and in trouble again. But this time it's the whole valley's trouble—killing trouble—and only Rock's blazing six-gun can stop it.

30,000 ON THE HOOF. Logan Huett, former scout for General Crook on his campaign into Apache territory, carries his innocent new bride off to a life in a lonely canyon where human and animal predators threaten his dream of raising a strong family and a magnificent herd.

Zane Grey is a true legend. His best selling novels have thrilled generations of readers with heart-and guts characters, hard shooting action, and high-plains panoramas. Zane Grey is the genuine article, the real spirit of the Old West.

Buy 4 or More and $ave

When you buy 4 or more books from Harper Paperbacks, the Postage and Handling is **FREE**.

MAIL TO: **Harper Collins Publishers
P. O. Box 588, Dunmore, PA 18512-0588**
Telephone: (800) 331-3761

**Visa and MasterCard holders—call
1-800-331-3761 for fastest service!**

Yes, please send me the Zane Grey Western adventures I have checked:
- ☐ The Rainbow Trail (0-06-100080-9) $3.50
- ☐ The Dude Ranger (0-06-100055-8) $3.50
- ☐ The Lost Wagon Train (0-06-100064-7) $3.50
- ☐ Wildfire (0-06-100081-7) $3.50
- ☐ The Man Of The Forest (0-06-100082-5) $3.50
- ☐ The Border Legion (0-06-100083-3) $3.50
- ☐ Sunset Pass (0-06-100084-1) $3.50
- ☐ 30,000 On The Hoof (0-06-100085-X) $3.50

SUBTOTAL . . . . $_____

POSTAGE AND HANDLING* . . . . $_____

SALES TAX (NJ, NY, PA residents) . . . . $_____

TOTAL: $_____
(Remit in US funds, do not send cash.)

Name_____

Address_____

City_____

State_____ Zip_____ Allow up to 6 weeks delivery. Prices subject to change.

*Add $1 postage/handling for up to 3 books...
FREE postage/handling if you buy 4 or more.

H0011

Saddle-up to these

THE REGULATOR *by Dale Colter*
Sam Slater, blood brother of the Apache and a cunning bounty-hunter, is out to collect the big price on the heads of the murderous Pauley gang. He'll give them a single choice: surrender and live, or go for your sixgun.

THE REGULATOR—Diablo At Daybreak
by Dale Colter
The Governor wants the blood of the Apache murderers who ravaged his daughter. He gives Sam Slater a choice: work for him, or face a noose. Now Slater must hunt down the deadly renegade Chacon...Slater's Apache brother.

THE JUDGE *by Hank Edwards*
Federal Judge Clay Torn is more than a judge—sometimes he has to be the jury *and* the executioner. Torn pits himself against the most violent and ruthless man in Kansas, a battle whose final verdict will judge one man right...and one man dead.

THE JUDGE—War Clouds
by Hank Edwards
Judge Clay Torn rides into Dakota where the Cheyenne are painting for war and the army is shining steel and loading lead. If war breaks out, someone is going to make a pile of money on a river of blood.

📚 HarperPaperbacks *By Mail*

5 great westerns!

THE RANGER *by Dan Mason*
Texas Ranger Lex Cranshaw is after a killer whose weapon isn't a gun, but a deadly noose. Cranshaw has vowed to stop at nothing to exact justice for the victims, whose numbers are still growing…but the next number up could be his own.

Here are 5 Western adventure tales that are as big as all outdoors! You'll thrill to the action and Western-style justice: swift, exciting, and man-to-man!

Buy 4 or more and save!
When you buy 4 or more books, the postage and handling is FREE!

VISA and MasterCard holders—call 1-800-331-3761 for fastest service!

MAIL TO: Harper Collins Publishers, P. O. Box 588, Dunmore, PA 18512-0588, Tel: (800) 331-3761

YES, send me the Western novels I've checked:

- ☐ **The Regulator**
  0-06-100100-7 . . . . $3.50
- ☐ **The Regulator/ Diablo At Daybreak**
  0-06-100140-6 . . . . $3.50
- ☐ **The Judge**
  0-06-100072-8 . . . $3.50
- ☐ **The Judge/War Clouds**
  0-06-100131-7 . . . . $3.50
- ☐ **The Ranger**
  0-06-100110-4 . . . . $3.50

SUBTOTAL . . . . $_____

POSTAGE AND HANDLING* . . . . $_____

SALES TAX (NJ, NY, PA residents) . . . . $_____

Remit in US funds, do not send cash

TOTAL: $_____

Name_____

Address_____

City_____

State_____ Zip_____

Allow up to 6 weeks delivery. Prices subject to change.

*Add $1 postage/handling for up to 3 books…
FREE postage/handling if you buy 4 or more.

H0131